TIGER MOM

A Romantic Suspense Novel

EVE LANGLAIS

PROLOGUE

THE NIGHT she witnessed Ronin murder his cousin—the blade he pulled from a pocket sliding with ease into Aroon—Macey knew she had to leave. Not because he'd killed someone. She'd always known he had a rough edge to him, the capacity for violence. Ronin hadn't become the head of his family because he followed the rules. It was one of the things that attracted her.

What she feared was how easily he could be provoked. He'd killed his favorite cousin, and for what? Because Aroon bought the same car as Ronin, down to the color.

Some people would have taken that as a compliment. Ronin saw it as Aroon trying to hedge in on his power base. His pride couldn't handle it.

So Ronin, without warning or chance of apology, killed his favorite cousin.

If he could do that to Aroon, what would he do to Macey? She'd rather leave before she found out.

But how could she escape? After two years of dating,

Ronin controlled almost every aspect of her life. From the apartment he set her up in, to ensuring that his driver took her to the research institute and back home.

As he often told her: *You belong to me.*

Once upon a time, Macey had thought those words exciting. Thrilling, to have a powerful man like Ronin paying her attention. Now, they resembled a threat.

Ronin turned from the slumping body, Aroon's eyes open in shock, his lips parting on one last sigh. Despite having killed someone, Ronin's expression and demeanor remained calm. She would wager that this wasn't his first time or even his second. Too nonchalant for that.

For Macey, though? It was a first, and her stomach churned.

This can't be happening. Aroon can't be dead.

While Macey had never particularly liked the man, he didn't deserve to die. Why would Ronin let her see him doing this?

This wasn't good.

Not good at all.

Macey kept her gaze from Aroon's chest where the red stain blossomed.

"That went better than expected."

"Better, how?" she almost bitterly exclaimed.

Ronin snapped his fingers and reminded her they weren't alone. Chen stood nearby—the equivalent of Ronin's right-hand man. Almost a business partner. Or, if looking at it with a more villainous bent, Chen the henchman.

"I hate it when they cry and whine." Silent until now,

Chen stepped forward from his spot by the doorway, entering into the otherwise sealed room.

A slender man dressed in a velvet tracksuit, navy blue with a white stripe, he reveled in his position as Ronin's most trusted associate. Which was the polite term. In reality, Chen worked for Ronin.

"Some people have no honor," Ronin agreed. He'd chosen to dress casually this evening in a designer knockoff of the bad boy image—jeans, strategically worn and ripped. An athletic and slim-fitting, short-sleeve tee in matte black. Over the top, a leather jacket—no colors, no markings. He didn't need to announce his name. People simply knew who Ronin was.

"You know what to do with it." Its edge glistening with blood, Ronin handed the murder weapon to Chen.

"Consider it done." Chen wrapped the knife in a cloth and then pulled out a plastic bag. That took a level of preparation that indicated premeditation. With the murder weapon tucked away, Chen nudged the body with a booted foot. "Full disappearance, or do you want him found as a lesson?" Chen spoke in English. All of Ronin's friends, family, and coworkers did when Macey was around. He'd said it would be rude to do otherwise, given that she didn't speak their language. She was learning slowly, though, enough that she caught hints of Ronin's true business. It wasn't just exporting cheap goods and drugs. Apparently, he was fond of weapons, too.

Repeat after me: Mob boyfriends are only hot in books. Once reality had set in, it became terrifying.

"Have him found. Publicly, if you can. Apparently, a

reminder is needed as to who is in charge and what happens to those who trespass against me."

Trespass? He'd murdered someone over a freaking car. She had to wonder what petty thing would set Ronin off next.

Maybe the way she chewed on her toast. He'd remarked upon it just last week. How about the fact that she hated swimming? Anything might be grounds for him to do the same thing to her.

I could die next. And she'd only have herself to blame.

Her stupidity practically slapped her. She'd seen the signs and ignored them. The way people didn't just defer to Ronin but feared him. The way his temper could flare, not loudly or violently, not with heated outbursts, but with cold precision. He knew just how to verbally cut so she'd apologize.

She'd been doing that a lot of late. He always made it seem so logical that she was in the wrong. Always wrong.

Too tired to go out? She obviously didn't value their time together. Didn't she love him?

Of course, I love you, Ronin. The words fell with familiarity from her lips. And they used to mean something. She'd loved him in the beginning.

Now, she had to wonder if something was wrong with her because how could she love such a cold monster?

In her defense, it seemed romantic in the books she read, the movies and shows she watched. Alpha males were assertive, commanding, even violent if tested. But not many could argue their sexiness.

Even now, she wouldn't deny Ronin's good looks. When she'd come to China from the US to study, her friends had tried to convince her that Asian men weren't hot.

She dared them to say that about Ronin. His body was a finely tooled example of physical perfection. Muscles honed. A few inches taller than she. His skin smooth.

But his better-than-average appearance didn't indicate his character.

Given the things she'd gleaned of late, she'd come to the startling and chilling conclusion that Ronin might be a psychopath. A narcissist for sure. Definitely a control freak. And a mobster. A rich and very powerful one. One who could kill his cousin, a guy he'd grown up with, and casually brush it off.

Where did that leave her?

She clenched her fists rather than hug herself. He'd notice. She didn't want him looking at her right now.

Chen grabbed the body, Aroon's face, a man she'd seen more than a few times, slack. Dead. She couldn't help it. Her gorge rose. She turned around and threw up. It wasn't pretty. And it lasted longer than it should have before her stomach ceased heaving.

Damn Ronin for being by her side, a hand on her back. Concerned.

"Just let it out," he soothed. "You'll feel better."

Except she didn't feel better. She felt worse as she wiped a hand across her mouth and straightened. It occurred to her that Ronin had an ulterior motive in bringing her to witness Aroon's death this evening. It was a warning to her.

See what happens if you don't keep me happy.

Macey had been picking petty squabbles with Ronin of late. Little things that thus far he'd let slide. How long before he retaliated?

It chilled to realize that he might hurt her. Hurt... She kept her gaze averted from her midsection. It had come as such a shock, and yet when she'd missed her period, something that had never happened since she'd started having one, she'd immediately bought the kit. Only hours ago, she'd spent a few tense minutes in the bathroom with a pee-covered stick.

She'd read the box twice to be sure of the results, then had buried the evidence of the pregnancy in a garbage bag, which she took to the chute down the hall of her building immediately after.

Pregnant. With Ronin's child.

I can't stay. This man should never be a daddy.

"I think I should go home and lie down." The truth, though? She didn't want to spend any time with Ronin but knew better than to say anything aloud. She'd end up with another three-hour lecture, being berated and explained to, passive-aggressively, how she'd let him down. How he tried so hard. How much he loved her.

Sometimes, she thought it would be quicker if Ronin just slapped her. A quick burst of pain, an apology, and it would be over.

Then that wish had become a reality, and she realized the stinging pain wasn't any better because it roused a burning shame inside her. She'd always been a girl to state that she'd never let a man hit her. A woman who considered herself equal to men. Yet when Ronin had left a mark on her flesh as punishment, she'd ended up being someone who apologized for her behavior. Then had sex with him.

How could she escape the vicious cycle?

"My love, of course, you need to rest. Come. My car is just outside." He placed a steadying—vise-tight—arm around her waist and walked her to the exit door where he'd parked the car by the warehouse on their way to dinner. Given it wasn't the first time he'd made this kind of stop, she'd thought nothing of it. More often than not, he left Macey in the car and popped inside for a few minutes. If he knew it would take longer, he sat her in his office, usually on his lap, while he dealt with issues in front of her. Brisk. Firm. Commanding. The sex on his desk after was always excellent but not worth the rest.

She had to wonder how many other times he'd killed and then nonchalantly rejoined her to enjoy a multi-course meal.

The car took them right to the condo, and Ronin escorted her upstairs. She couldn't fault his manners. Always courteous. Technically, the perfect boyfriend. So, why did she scream so often inside her head?

They entered the large condo—the penthouse, of course. Only the best for his love. When Macey had first arrived in China on a research grant, she'd been living in a tiny apartment where she could practically cook from her bed. Then she'd met Ronin at a function given by the company that she worked for.

They fell hard and fast for each other. Soon, he

moved her out of her cramped place and paid for everything. Since he had a key, Ronin came and went as he pleased. Mostly, he stayed with Macey, sometimes spending the night on the couch with her just watching movies—hopping away every so often to deal with business. Other times, he joined her in the kitchen to cook.

And he was supportive when it came to the work she did at the institute. As a newly graduated scientist, she worked hard to make her mark.

So what if her boyfriend killed people who annoyed him or got in his way? The movies claimed he was sexy.

Now, he scared her and posed a threat to the baby growing inside her.

I have to leave.

The thought had gotten persuasive when, about three months ago, his mask had slipped for a moment. He'd said something sharp and cruel to her: *"You should count yourself lucky I chose you over others who could bring me more status."* And the reason for the insult? She'd wanted to work late in the lab rather than join him for a party.

He'd apologized profusely and skipped the gala, bringing her food and flowers. Manipulation. She knew it then, knew it more now, and yet it generally seemed easier to go with the flow.

Ronin moved for the fridge. He kept it stocked for her. Stocked for his girlfriend.

His mistress.

Or as a few of the eligible ladies had hissed to Macey, his whore.

Rather than pull out a bottle of wine or something with liquor, he chose some fancy, bubbly soda. The top popped, and he poured some into two fluted glasses, the foam rising and stopping just before the rim. Ronin handed her one and lifted the other.

"Are we celebrating something?" she asked, trepidation making the words slightly quiver.

"We will be. Look inside your glass." His lips held a hint of a smile. What had he done now?

The foam cleared, and a peek at the bottom of her drink showed a ring. Her stomach clenched. Oh, no.

The nightmare compounded.

Ronin dipped to one knee. "Marry me." No flowery speech accompanied the demand. When it came to the most important things, Ronin believed in being direct.

She knew the answer he expected. The one he wanted. Yet that symbol on the stick she'd peed on changed everything. She had to at least try.

"I don't know if I'm ready."

Nothing marred his expression. It remained steady as Ronin stared at her. "Not ready."

Not even a question, yet she babbled to expand her reply. "I'm barely out of school, and I've still got at least a year left of work on my contract."

"I know." No context. Nothing but a flat stare that went from her face to her stomach.

Everything in her froze. He couldn't know. She'd just found out. He was guessing. Yet there was something in his gaze... Certainty and patience as he waited to hear her lie.

How would he know if she lied?

The realization blossomed. How could she have been so blind? "You've been spying on me!"

He didn't even try to deny it. "The condo comes with many enhanced security features that allow monitoring of every room."

"And you've been watching me?"

"We live together, what exactly don't I see already? Do you have secrets, my love?" Spoken as a deadly threat.

Oh, God. He'd seen her that morning. Knew...

Her gaze flitted to the ceiling in her place, the pictures, the furniture. All this time, everything she'd done, he'd been watching.

"You had no right," she huffed. She couldn't help the anger, even as she braced for his reply.

"I own you." Three words that didn't sound so hot right now.

"No, you don't." She found her inner strength and defied him, bolstering her courage with the thought of what she now had to protect.

"Actually, I do. You carry something of mine." He stood and placed his free hand on her belly, which contracted.

It almost occurred to her to declare that it wasn't his. But that might be worse.

"I just found out. I was going to tell you once I confirmed it with a doctor. Make the announcement special." She sought the words to diffuse the coldness in his gaze.

"I'm sure you were. But, my love, I can't let you go through this alone. I will be with you every step of our child's journey."

The nightmare worsened. "We shouldn't go crazy yet. I haven't even seen a doctor or anything."

"Nor have you replied to my proposal. You do want to marry me, right, my love?"

"This all seems so fast." She wavered on her feet and could feel her heart racing, the panic very real.

"How is this fast? We've been together for a while. Marriage is the next step." He stared at her, and she knew the correct reply.

But her stomach churned, and she couldn't say it. The panic in her swelled, quick and uncontained.

Instead, she blurted, "I can't marry you."

"Why?"

If she listed the reasons, he'd kill her. And the baby. She placed a hand over her belly. "The only reason you're marrying me is because you think I am carrying your child. What if you find out I'm not, and the test was wrong?"

"I would still marry you. Because I love you. Don't you love me?"

There was a deadly dare in his stare. A challenge to reject him one more time and see what happened.

"Of course, I love you." She faked the best smile of her life. The one that would win her awards if she acted. "It would be my deepest honor to marry you."

"Only honored?"

She hid her swallow behind a smile as she said, "I meant pleasure. I can't wait to be your wife."

"And a father." He clinked her glass with the other. "We will marry, and soon."

"How soon?" she asked.

"Soon enough that no one will dare call my child a bastard."

"Does it really matter in this day and age?" she said lightly.

"It does to me." He gripped her chin, hard enough that she'd notice bruises the next day. "Now, toast with me. This is a wondrous day, my love."

No, it was the start of a nightmare. That same evening, she became a virtual prisoner, only allowed to leave the house while with Ronin or under guard. Clearly, he was taking no chances with his new wife.

Yes, wife. He'd gotten his way within forty-eight hours. Mostly because the person officiating didn't care if she actually mumbled an assent. She'd worn a white lace gown, and he a tux. The female guests scowled the whole time.

Within the week, Ronin had her seeing an obstetrician on a regular basis. At the first ultrasound, he left bragging of his virility when they discovered that Macey carried twins. He restricted her activities even further. Assigned a guard to her, then two.

It was during her second trimester, on her way to a doctor's appointment, that it happened.

The doors to the elevator had almost shut when fingers slid between them and popped them apart. Chen bristled and made to act, only to settle down when a woman with dark skin, her hair tucked in a tight chignon, wearing a smart suit, entered the elevator with them. She held a phone to her ear and spoke in English, "Call you back, getting on the elevator." She reached forward and pressed for the top floor.

Chen, behind and to her left, ogled her bum and mimed grabbing it to hump, while Tao, the other babysitting guard, smirked. And they wondered why they were single.

Pigs, both of them, but not when it came to Macey. While they might not like the fact that they'd been assigned babysitting duty, they respected Ronin's wife—everyone remembered what'd happened to Kyle.

Kyle had only said something complimentary about her smile. Ronin didn't handle his jealousy well. Rumor had it that when the police came to see him at the hospital, he'd written on a pad that he'd sewn his mouth shut himself.

Chen, in Mandarin, said, "Think she gags or takes it like a pro?"

A rude query, to which Tao chuckled.

The woman suddenly turned, her ruby red lips curving into a smile. "Is that any way to treat a lady?" she asked in perfect Mandarin before shooting them both.

Bang. Bang. The shots were muffled by the short silencer. The bodies collapsed, and Macey's jaw dropped open.

Oh, shit.

She retreated until she smacked the rear wall of the elevator. "Please don't kill me," she pled as she cupped her very rounded belly.

"Don't freak. I'm here to rescue you. That is assuming you want to leave your husband."

"This is a trick," Macey said, shaking her head. "Another one of his tests." Ronin enjoyed playing games with people. And then punishing them if they failed.

"I promise, this is no joke. I can get you out of China and away from his influence."

Oh, how she wanted to believe, but she'd lost hope months ago. She shook her head. "Ronin will never let me go." It wouldn't matter how far she ran; he'd find her.

"Do you really think he'll hold on to a dead woman?"

The chilling statement had her trembling. "I don't want to die."

The woman snorted. "I'm not actually going to kill you. Just make him think I did." She winked. "Trust me, I am good at what I do." The elevator kept rising, past the floor for her doctor.

"Who are you?"

"My friends call me Marie. I'm a problem solver, especially for women like you."

"Like me?"

Her face turned serious. "Caught in a terrible situation with no way out."

"You have to stop talking. If Ronin hears any of this, he will kill you."

"First, he'd have to find me. And who says I won't kill him first. Come with me." The elevator stopped on the very top floor, and the door opened. Marie stepped on the seam between the cab and the floor, hands spread enough to hold the doors ajar.

Macey hesitated. What if this was a trick? He would punish her.

Then again, every day, every hour, every *minute* was punishment. Would she subject her babies to the same treatment? They deserved better.

She placed her hand on her baby bump. "How much will this rescue cost me?"

"No more than you can give. The people I work for can protect you."

The statement roused her suspicion. "What people?"

"Secret ones. Powerful. Rich. Connected. We can make it so Ronin never touches you or the babies," Marie added softly.

"If you really wanted to help me, then you would kill him."

"We will certainly try, but as you've noticed, he's well protected."

"And vengeful."

The elevator doors tried to shut but bounced back open.

"I need you to decide," the woman declared. "Are you staying with him or coming with me?"

Macey's phone went off in her purse. She knew that ringtone. Hated it.

Ronin called.

Did Ronin watch her even now?

Macey eyed the bodies at her feet.

This stranger was a killer, and yet she offered a way out.

Macey nodded. "Help me."

The helicopter alit the moment the door to the rooftop shut. Marie kept her promise.

That same day, Macey disappeared, kidnapped by persons unknown, only to die in a fiery helicopter crash. Dead and burned to a crisp.

Or so everyone believed.

Meanwhile, a whole continent away, Portia Stalone was born. She spent the next few years at the Canadian

Killer Moms training compound with her twins, born at thirty-five weeks, five pounds two ounces, and six pounds one ounce, respectively. Lin and Mae. Her reasons for living.

When they turned two, she was moved to a suburb in Toronto and commuted into town a few times a week to work in a medical facility that Marie finagled a position for her in.

Eventually, Macey relocated to a bigger place in the United States with a fully-funded private lab run by some pharmaceutical company, less bound by Canadian laws. It provided her the cover she needed to play with cool machines and create neat concoctions.

Macey spent the decade following her escape paying back Killer Moms for saving her life.

CHAPTER ONE

PICKING the twins up from their private school, Portia noticed a dichotomy. All the kids milling in the yard and on the sidewalks were doing something: bouncing a ball, chatting with friends, shoving each other, or chasing. Not her girls.

Much like the twins in *The Shining*, they stood side by side in their identical uniforms, alone and looking unnervingly tidy alongside their peers. At only nine years of age, they shouldn't be so serious.

When was the last time she'd seen them play with childish abandon? What about exercise? Surely, it wasn't healthy for them to be reading and on the computer all of the time.

Then again, she'd had her face stuck in a book at that age too. Still, as she noticed the separation between them and the other children, she couldn't help an anxious spurt of worry that wondered if she parented them wrong. Was she failing at motherhood?

Impossible. She'd read all the instructions. So many

tomes of knowledge. She'd applied the techniques she liked most to great success. Just look at their accomplishments. Speaking in full sentences by the age of one. Walking before that. Potty trained by two. Reading before they even went into kindergarten. As a matter of fact, scholastically, her brilliant daughters were a few years ahead of the other children their age. Socially, though, they appeared to be lacking.

Portia had obviously forgotten what it was like to be the smart kid in school. The way other kids had shunned her because she actually enjoyed learning. Because of her social awkwardness, Portia had eschewed friendship for lonely pursuits. It wasn't too late for her daughters. Mae and Lin had each other, at least, but they needed more than that.

Of late, she'd noticed the girls getting terse with each other, the uncanny closeness stifling. Mae at least appeared to be chafing. The fights were coming more frequently. They'd even decided to inhabit separate rooms for the first time. Mae didn't even wait until Portia had painted the guest bedroom before moving her stuff in.

The separation between the two didn't result in either of her girls getting out and socializing more. They needed friends. At the very least, a hobby that didn't involve studying.

On the drive home, she saw the solution to getting them out of the house and not only meeting new kids but also getting exercise, all while learning a skill. Multitasking at its finest. Not that she mentioned that. Instead, she presented it as a practical thing.

"You want us to learn to kickbox?" Mae said with a wrinkle of her nose.

"I don't want anyone to hit me," Lin added, just as repugned.

"Martial arts are about learning how to protect yourself," Portia encouraged. "It will be fun."

"How is getting hematomas fun?" Mae, the child of big words—that she could not only pronounce but also spell.

"I'll bet it's gross and sweaty." The pout on Lin's lips actually made her seem her age.

"You have to try it at least once," Portia replied. It was one of her parental rules. They had to give something a proper chance before she'd agree to let them quit. Food, activity, even movies.

"Once. And if I get hurt, then I get ice cream," Lin declared. She had a sweet tooth, that Portia hadn't succeeded in curbing.

"She's going to let herself get smacked on purpose," Mae declared. "Just so she can stuff her fat face."

"As if I'd intentionally gain weight," sniffed Lin. "If I do eat some sweets, I'll do a little extra cardio on the stairs at home."

"Might want to double that now that you're drinking coffee in the morning," Mae tattled.

"Lin! You told me it was hot chocolate," Portia hotly declared.

"Not exactly. I called it hot mocha. You assumed the wrong kind of beans."

Portia gripped the wheel. Outsmarted again. It stung, mostly because she'd thought herself pretty intelligent until she became a parent. Apparently, they had an answer for everything.

"We're here." Portia pulled into the plaza where she'd seen the sign. Flamingo Martial Arts decorated with a pink bird in sunglasses balancing on a single leg, wearing a headband, and a black belt. Surely, that made it child-friendly. Right?

The girls were silent in the back. Too quiet. Portia had learned early on that silence didn't bode well. It was true what they said: twins could communicate, and they did so often to plot. The first real scary silence had occurred the time they escaped their crib, Lin giving Mae a boost. When they were younger, the girls had always relied on each other. Always worked as a team. As a mother, Portia had to be doubly careful to not let them outnumber her. Add age and cunning...the thought of their teenage years terrified her.

Especially since they'd never really been children to start with.

Did I push them too hard?

Portia parked and unbuckled before turning around and brightly saying, "Ready to check it out?"

"We'd rather jab each other with sharp sticks," Mae declared. Her penchant for the color blue—blue jeans and pale blue sweatshirts, or navy blue jumpers with an offsetting white shirt—went well with her dark and morbid streak. Aunt Joanna, the one who minded them while Portia worked, enjoyed antagonizing Mae by calling her Wednesday Adams.

It fit. Now, if only she could find a Gomez.

"You haven't even given martial arts a try. How do you know you won't like it?"

Lin tilted her head. She was the very girly, preppy twin, with her long hair combed into a straight sheen, and her lip gloss always freshly applied. When had her girls gone from child to pre-teen? It felt like she'd blinked and...bam, they were growing up way too fast. She needed to reel them back. Make them into children again, at least for a few more years.

"You told us we're not supposed to hit people," Lin reminded.

"Yes, well. Um." Portia exited the car and thought quickly of a reply. Her twins often did this, using Portia's own words against her. She opened the rear passenger door. "You should know how to defend yourself in case you're attacked."

"Why would someone attack us? We know not to go to bad places." Said with all the eye-rolling arrogance of youth.

"But that's just it, bad places can happen anywhere. Which is why you should be prepared." It was the best argument Portia could offer.

Little miss Wednesday Adams had a smirk as she said, "Then maybe you should have some lessons too, Mother. We wouldn't want you to be unprotected."

Lin hopped right in on that. "Yes, Mother Dear. If we must learn to hit things, then we should do it together."

The manipulation proved most obvious, and she could have easily countered by telling the twins that she'd already taken lessons and could probably put any teacher on his ass. But rather than fight it, Portia saw a chance to spend time with her girls. "You're right. I should be prepared, too. I think this is a great idea. The Stalone girls, taking a class together." She smiled as she wrenched open the door, setting off the little bell.

They walked into a small reception area with tile floors and a shoe rack with a sign. *Please remove all outdoor footwear.* The rest of the open space consisted of cushioned mats, while the mirrored walls lined with bars reflected the room and its occupants. It resembled, in some respects, a dance studio.

Someone appeared to be crouched behind the counter, only the shaggy top of a head showing.

"Give me just a second," rumbled the man, his voice deep.

Portia set her purse down on the counter and waited as he finished tucking something away in a cabinet. When he rose to face them, Portia blinked.

"Ted?" Her lips clamped tight, too late to take it back.

The man with the chiseled jaw covered in a thin beard glanced at her, no recognition in his gaze at first. That only lasted a second before his eyes widened. "Macey? Holy crow, I didn't recognize you for a second there. You changed your hair. It's been a long time."

She almost bit her lower lip as he used her old name. Her *before* name, which her daughters must have heard and yet, neither said a word. She wouldn't make a big deal about it, not in their hearing range at any rate.

"Yeah, I haven't seen you since our senior year." They'd both graduated at the same time, her with honors.

"You went off to university, didn't you? On some scholarship."

"Yes." Then she went on to work for a medical institute doing cutting-edge things. Which was where she'd met the wrong man, and things went downhill.

"Did you graduate?"

"Do I seem like the type who wouldn't?" she asked with an arched brow.

He made a face. "Sorry. That didn't come out right. Of course, you became a doctor."

"I did." She kept her answers short and clipped. She needed to get out of here and quickly before Ted said something she couldn't explain to her daughters.

"These your girls?" he asked, resting his gaze on them. "Hi. I'm Ted," he said, holding out his hand to her solemn Wednesday first.

Her daughter shook it and eyed him. "Mae."

Lips pursed, and dimple showing, Lin practically shoved her aside to grab his hand next. "And I'm the cute one, Lin. Mother brought us to your lovely dojo to sign us up for lessons."

Lovely? What was happening here? Her daughters, being nice? Even more reason to leave.

"I was going to register, but looking at your schedule, it appears as if those beginner classes are at the same time as piano." Portia only partially lied. The twins had piano, but they could easily work Ted's classes around it.

Mae tittered. Actually *tittered* as she said, "Oh, Mother. Piano is on Tuesday. We can still come Monday, Wednesday, and Friday."

"Maybe even Saturday," Lin hastened to add, batting her lashes.

Portia regarded her suddenly too-keen daughters,

both of them staring at Ted. Handsome Ted, the football player, whom all the girls wanted to date in high school. He'd asked her out once, but she'd turned him down to study for a test. Which she'd aced. Perhaps if she'd been more social and dated a bit more, she'd have had the savviness required to not fall for Ronin's lies.

"I don't know. Maybe this isn't a good idea. I know how Lin feels about possibly getting hit in the face. And Mae doesn't like to sweat." Portia used their previous excuses to try and get out of it.

"Mother!" Lin exhaled with annoyance.

"She's chickening out," Mae declared. And then she clucked.

Which proved embarrassing but not as much as realizing that she was being a coward. Seeing someone from her past could result in danger. But only if he told someone about her. Who would he tell? They'd barely known each other in high school. He'd obviously moved from their small town.

To whom would he blow her cover? Even if he told his mom, or a buddy back home. So what? It wasn't as if it would get back to Ronin. For one, he wasn't even looking for her. It had been almost a decade since her fake death. He'd moved on.

There was no danger. She had to stop worrying all the time.

This studio was convenient, smack dab between the girls' academy and their house. Not to mention, her daughters needed to do something. How better to get them interested than with a teacher they were both eyeballing like that science experiment in the tub last semester.

I can't live in fear forever. And Ted was still rather cute.

Portia smiled. "How do we sign up?"

He pushed a clipboard in her direction. "Just fill this out." As she printed in the blanks, the girls slipped off their shoes and wandered to a display case filled with trophies.

He felt a need to make idle chit-chat. "So, whatcha doing these days? Working at the hospital?"

"Not quite. I'm a researcher for a private clinic."

"And your husband?"

She shot him a glance. "What makes you think I'm married? Just because I have children? Or because a woman shouldn't be raising them alone?" She'd heard it all in the past decade. Misguided commentary on how she should live her life. She was perfectly fine on her own. She barely had time for herself with her daughters' busy schedule, and her work.

He chuckled, a deep baritone that almost brought a shiver. "Don't get all twisted in a knot. I was just asking because of the name." He pointed to the Stalone. He'd known her as Munroe.

"I am a widow and kept my husband's last name for the girls." Which would explain part of her name change on the form. "And I'm going by my middle name these days. Never did like my old one."

"Fair enough. Portia." He tested it out. "Will you be the only one coming with the girls?"

"I just told you I was widowed."

"I caught that. I was only wondering if you'll have someone else responsible for dropping them off and picking them up. A nanny, family member, friend."

"Actually, Mother will be taking lessons with us," Mae declared, having wandered back in their direction.

Lin jumped in. "Because a woman should know how to defend herself."

"Man or woman. Everyone should be able to stand up for themselves," Ted remarked. "I think it's great you're doing this as a family."

This whole situation had gotten out of hand quickly, and Portia couldn't see a way out of it. She'd told the girls she'd do it. But should she do this with Ted? He created an unnecessary link to her past. Posed a danger if he opened his mouth.

She should walk out and try somewhere else.

Instead, she managed a smile and said, "We'd like three memberships, please."

She kept that pleasant expression and dulcet tone even as she finished the registration process. Wore the smile the entire drive back to their house. They had time for a nutritious dinner, then homework. Not that her girls actually had any. They went to a private school that had an adaptive method of teaching and learning that let the students set their own pace. The twins happened to give themselves strict guidelines and were very disciplined. What could Portia say? The girls took after her and excelled academically.

Around eight o'clock, Aunt Joanna arrived to mind the twins. A woman in her sixties, Joanna was round-cheeked with frizzy hair that ran the gamut of gray to white. Her figure appeared bulky, and she always smelled like lavender. What no one saw under the thick cardigan was the muscle she'd built over the decades, or the knives strapped to her thighs in case the gun at her back wasn't enough.

A decade of peace and quiet didn't mean Portia ever grew too complacent. Ronin wasn't the only thing she watched for.

Portia worked for some very important people. Those who sometimes acted in ways that made other powerful groups angry. Given Portia often helped them achieve their goals, she could end up targeted one day.

More than once, she'd thought of quitting. But quitting meant being on her own without the extended family she'd found with Marie—her handler and de facto mother—and the others—sisters by choice. All of them single mothers, bound together by tough pasts, forged into an agency that worked to make the world a better place—for the right price. Portia could thank Ronin for showing her that sometimes death was necessary. She'd come to realize that the removal of one key player could often save many.

But who got to decide was the part of the equation that Portia still struggled with. The missions Portia enjoyed the most were those that didn't involve killing but still got the job done. Abrupt confessions. Chemical castration. Head to toe, intense itching every time a certain rapist even had a sexual thought.

"Off to work again?" Aunt Joanna asked.

"Yes. I want to check the results on some tests I started earlier today."

"You work too hard." A statement she heard all too often.

"I never miss a thing with the girls." But in between driving them around for their activities, and spending quality time conversing about their days, she crammed in every extra second of work that she could.

"You're an excellent mother. Pity you're not so intense about your own needs."

"What are you talking about? I'm perfectly satisfied."

Joanna snorted. "The sad part is you don't even realize what you're missing out on. Don't be me. Live your life before you're too old to enjoy it."

"I'm living just fine. See you in a few hours." Portia left and headed to her lab. Yes, hers. The pharmaceutical company had given her an entire floor with staff because she was a valuable asset. Which meant she got carte blanche to do whatever she liked. Little did they know she sometimes did work for the secret agency that'd rescued her.

She had to slow when she reached the security gate. Only for a moment before she got waved through. The guards in the place had gotten used to her coming and going at all hours. A keycard got her into the building and set the elevator in motion. The high-tech structure had all kinds of electronic controls to keep out non-employees. It also believed in watching every move their employees made, which was why when Portia entered her space, she triggered a special code that would play doctored footage of her actions. In other words, play a deep fake to act as camouflage, masking what she was really doing.

Only once she had on her white jacket and sat on her

stool did she voice activate the KM virtual system. "Tiger Mom, authorization Alpha Niner Gamma Two." Recognizing her vocal pattern and code, the screen playing a spinning version of the company logo faded and turned into that of KM Realty, which was the cover for Killer Moms.

Most of the mothers, picked up from desperate situations like Portia, worked for KM in mundane positions that involved paint chips and fabric swatches. But a few had special skills better used elsewhere. Such as Portia, who could concoct just about any potion or serum needed.

The screen pulsed with an incoming transmission.

"Accept the call."

The screen filled with gray, a wall to be exact, plain with not a single feature to be seen. Marie wasn't one to compromise her safety, even on secure channels. She stepped in front of the camera, still as beautiful as the day she'd rescued Portia.

"Hello, Portia. It's been a while."

"Has it? I thought we had dinner at Easter."

"Six months ago. But not entirely your fault. I've been meaning to visit, but things have been busy. How are you and the girls?" Marie asked.

"Doing well, thanks. I signed them up for martial arts classes."

Marie's lips rounded. "Does Lin know it involves hitting?"

"Yes." Portia's lips curved. "And they were planning to talk their way out of it until they met the instructor."

"Handsome boy?"

"Handsome man," she corrected, recalling his broad physique. The face had lost its boyish softness to the chiseled planes of adulthood.

"Must be good-looking if you noticed."

"Oh, I noticed, all right. He hasn't changed a bit since high school." Her lips turned down.

"You know him from before?" Marie's expression hardened. "Has your cover been compromised?"

She shook her head. "I don't think so. He remembers me, obviously as Macey, but he seemed to accept my explanation about why my name is different."

"Doesn't matter. You know there's a chance he could tell someone from your old town that he ran into you," Marie reminded.

"Only if he's in touch with anyone. Is it really a big deal if he tells his mom?"

"I am not taking a chance. We'll begin monitoring him immediately. What's his name?"

"Ted Grady. Works at the Flamingo Martial Arts place on Queen Street."

"Noted. Now, just in case he poses a problem, I'll begin scouting possible locations for you."

Her nose wrinkled. "Not a new place." When she'd moved here two years ago, the girls had been quite vocal in their displeasure.

"Better safe." Because if for one moment Ronin realized that Portia wasn't dead...

"I should just kill him," she sighed. Not an easy thing to say. Once upon a time, she'd loved the man. His children were the most precious things in her world, and he posed the biggest danger. Despite having the means at her disposal, she'd yet to take that final, fatal step to remove him forever.

"Say the word," Marie offered.

"Only if he becomes a problem." So long as Ronin thought them gone, they were safe. Everyone could just live their lives.

"I think we should handle this Ted person before he becomes an issue." Marie offered the simplest solution, just not the most palatable one.

"We are not killing Ted. He hasn't done anything wrong." There were some lines Portia wouldn't cross, and Marie respected them. Mostly. However, Portia also knew that Marie wouldn't hesitate to act if Ted posed a danger to one of her adopted daughters.

"Hopefully, things stay that way. Now, on to the real reason for my call. We need more of that truth serum you whipped up last year."

"Easy enough."

"There's a catch. It won't be easy to apply. We'll only have a narrow window of opportunity."

"How narrow?"

"The length of time it takes to get from the elevator to a courtroom a hundred paces away."

Rather than exclaim about the impossibility, her mind went to work. Portia rolled her chair to her smart board to take notes. "Do we have access to food or drink?"

"No."

She scribbled some more. "Skin-to-skin contact?"

"Difficult."

"But not impossible. Meaning, you can get someone within a few feet of the target?"

"Yes. I think so. But, at best, probably only for seconds."

A challenge for her skill set. "I'll work on something and get back to you. How soon do you need it?"

"The cartel trial happens in six weeks. We need a confession while they're on the stand."

"Let me see what I can do."

Portia already had something that would probably work, but *probably* wasn't a sure thing. She needed to test a delivery system, yet instead, she found herself online doing a search on Ted Grady.

She didn't find much. No social media. No newspaper articles. Nothing.

Odd in this day and age. She couldn't even discover if he'd married. Did he have kids? A significant other in his life?

Given her level of distraction, she was back home just after midnight and fell asleep thinking of Ted. In her dream, she didn't say no when he asked her to go to the dance. Instead, she wore a hideous pink lace dress that he said looked lovely. They slowly waltzed in circles inside the school gym. Then he took her to a spot under the bleachers for a kiss.

She woke sweaty and aching between her legs for the first time in a long while. Interested in a man. And why not? She hadn't hooked up with anyone since Ronin. If Ted were single—

Oh, God. She'd become the worst kind of cliché. Falling for a handsome instructor who happened to be a boy she kind of crushed on in school. A man who posed a danger. She should cancel the contract to take his classes. Or just not show up.

She had all kinds of reasons to not see him. But what did she tell her girls when they asked at breakfast?

"We'll try and hit their beginner class before dinner."

And their tandem reply, "Excellent."

It should have come with ominous music.

CHAPTER TWO

AFTER MACEY—*SORRY, Portia*—had left, Ted had to wonder at the weird circumstances that had brought them together. He'd thought her so hot in high school. She used to wear these tight jeans and had the sweetest ass in them. The serious girl, always studying and acing tests. So fucking smart. He really liked that about her.

She was so smart she'd turned him down the one time he'd gotten up the nerve to ask her out. Then she went off to university, whereas he'd enlisted, along with the other jocks who didn't get a scholarship and had no interest in acquiring a huge student loan.

It boggled the mind the odds of her showing up in his studio, ten years later, looking just as serious as he recalled, and still very attractive. But to his surprise, she had kids. He'd have wagered that she was too driven to stop for motherhood. In any case, it didn't appear to have softened her.

Her aloofness only increased her attractiveness. Should he ask her out? She was, after all, single. At the same time, he had no real interest in anything long-term, whereas she had kids to think of. She probably would not be interested in anything casual.

Or would she prefer someone who didn't want any strings tying them down? Could be she might want something casual and carnal.

Wishful thinking that would have to wait. A wave of students arrived, snapping him back to the present. He spent the next few hours running the different levels through the motions. Teaching them not only the soothing nature of the movements, but the confidence they needed to be able to stand up for themselves.

Since he'd opened the dojo, he'd had a stream of people sign up for his classes. The ones he took the most pleasure in were the shy ones, the meek students who wanted to feel more confident but lacked the mindset to do so. He liked teaching them to control that fear. Showing them that they could be as strong as they chose.

About half an hour after the last student had left, the sensor for his door beeped, letting him know someone had entered. Could be a late-night signup. Or a druggie looking to score a few quick bucks.

Ted turned from his cleaning of the mats to see three men walk in. Two of them Asian in features, the third Caucasian, his skin pockmarked, head shaved on the sides.

They belonged to the Evening Swords, a gang that owned this section of town, promising protection if properly paid. Terrorizing those that didn't.

It appeared they were collecting early this month.

Ted rose, barefoot and weaponless, unlike the trio.

Their leader, who went by the name Taotie, wore a loose tracksuit that could hide any number of weapons. He was rather partial to knives. Ralph, whose Asian features contrasted sharply with his dirty blond, curly hair, had a bulge by his ribs—a gun, most likely. The third was new and wide-eyed eager. The worst kind.

"Hello, gentlemen. How can I help you this evening?" Ted asked politely, well aware of how things worked with the Evening Swords. Lots of bluster interspersed with threats, followed by extortion.

Taotie spread his hands. "It's collection time."

"It's only the eleventh of the month. You usually come on the fifteenth."

"I'm busy the fifteenth." Taotie snapped his fingers. "Pay up."

"I don't have it." The wrong answer.

A smirk tugged Taotie's lips. "You're the third person to tell me that tonight. Would you like to know what I told them?"

Judging by the bruised knuckles on Ralph and the new kid? *Don't expect any leniency.*

Much as it stuck in his craw, Ted remained meek. He'd long ago learned that cutting off the head of the local snake only spawned a meaner one. "I can have it for you tomorrow. I never keep that kind of cash around."

"I think he just implied we don't give him proper protection," the kid stated.

"Why, I do believe you're right," Taotie's lips twisted into a sneer. "Perhaps karate man needs a lesson in how well we do our job."

Sigh. So much for avoiding it. Ted didn't tense at the

first blow, he let it land, fully aware they had to feel as if they'd gotten their piece. They punched, and he just defended, absorbing the worst, and faking pain before falling to a knee when a blow to his lip split it. Barely a flesh wound, but all the blood tended to impress people. He spat a red wad on the mat by Taotie's feet.

"Not so cocky now, are you?" Taotie taunted. "We'll be back tomorrow. Have the money, or else."

Ted would have it. Mostly because he considered it a cost of doing business.

Less than ten minutes later, after the gang had left, he locked the door and went upstairs to where he had converted a second-floor storage space into an actual apartment. He'd even installed a bathroom and a small kitchenette area.

Not the height of luxury, but he didn't have many needs. The big, comfy chair that creaked when he sat was one of his few splurges. The cold beer going down his throat another. The third and most expensive thing he owned, was the computer on the table in front of him. As the machine booted, he held a pack of frozen fries to his cheekbone, minimizing the hematoma he felt forming. Luckily, he didn't bruise like a peach. He had some friends who used to turn purple at even a hint of violence.

The computer login screen appeared, and he typed, the setup much more elaborate than anything else he owned. Because for him, having a powerful machine he could play on at home was worth the cost.

Ted wasn't much on going out. He'd seen the world. It was ugly. Every day, he could see signs of it online. The killing. The hate. The lies. He kept as far away from it as he could. It made it easier to hold his temper in check. Easier to fight the temptation of the vices that flooded the streets.

Once Ted logged in, he activated a private VPN that routed his signal via too many channels for anyone to follow. He protected himself before doing anything that might be considered shady.

Being a bit of a shut-in meant that he learned how to dig, deep enough to unearth secrets. He set off some searches, using some macros he'd programmed. They all went crawling, looking for Macey Munroe on the big, wide web. It didn't take long to realize that the Macey he once knew didn't exist. Not a single peep about the girl he'd known in high school, who'd gone off to do incredible medical things.

Who now went by another name.

But something niggled at him. He remembered hearing something back in the day on one of the rare occasions that he'd come home on leave. Something important regarding Macey.

Since normal searches weren't netting him anything, Ted dove past the regular internet most people knew, right into the dark web. The *real* internet.

He opened a new search window and typed in her name. For a price, he could access all kinds of databases, like that of his old high school. He found himself in those records, and other people whose names he remembered, but no Macey. Impossible. They'd graduated together.

More digging revealed that not only her school file was gone but also her birth records. Everything appeared to have vanished, except for one odd mention in a dark web forum devoted to archived newspapers. Buried inside a short paragraph of an ex-pat periodical circulated in Asia, a mention of the tragic demise of an American scientist in China.

Macey Munroe. Dead in a helicopter crash. Now, he remembered it. His mother had been quite excited, her whole church abuzz with the news. Could they have been wrong? Perhaps the clipping was about someone with the same name.

He swigged his beer and recalled how he'd almost not recognized her. Might not have clued in had she not used his name. She'd changed her hair. No longer strawberry blond, she'd gone brown and let it grow out from the shoulder-length she used to have. Then there was the mole on her jaw. A distinctive dark mark that he used to fantasize about kissing. It was now gone. As were the cute wire-rimmed glasses she used to wear. He also could have sworn that her nose and chin were different. A little more pointed.

But, people aged and changed their style. What he found a bit odder was that she'd changed her name. And lied about it. Portia wasn't her middle name. Nor was there any record of a Macey Munroe getting married. Not in North America or anywhere he could search marriage registries online.

However, there were a few places he couldn't get in to, countries with much more robust firewalls to penetrate. Hadn't the article mentioned that the helicopter crash had happened in China?

Interesting how she had two little girls with Asian features.

There were only a few reasons why someone would want to disappear. All of them deadly. In her case, he'd wager a mother on the run from an abusive ex. She had the look. Surprised to see him, then wary, as if worried that he'd rat her out. Ted would never do that. He preferred to help women find their confidence after some asshole took it from them. Then, at one point, when the demons inside his head got too loud, he sometimes made sure those assholes were taught a lesson about beating on others.

Given the whole change in name, she might be in some kind of witness protection program. She was a scientist. She could very well be testifying against a pharmaceutical company. They had deep enough pockets to make life dangerous for those who thought to spill their secrets.

The many reasons she might want to be someone else had him drumming his fingers on the desk and hesitating. However, he wasn't a man to leave a mystery alone. He was protected behind his layered firewalls. No one would know of his interest. He typed in Portia Stalone.

To his surprise, a litany of data surfaced. A full background, including schooling back to kindergarten, her driver's license, social media. She had a full and well-documented history. Especially for someone who hadn't been born with that name...

Odd.

And he knew just the type of people who would be interested in that kind of oddity.

CHAPTER THREE

A TIRED PORTIA sucked back coffee as she read Mother's overnight surveillance report. Turned out Ted resided where he worked. While they couldn't be one hundred percent sure he hadn't left, given a lack of cameras in the area, cellphone pings showed Ted not moving from his building. He didn't call or text anyone, just hopped on the internet and watched Youtube fishing videos for a few hours.

Boring. Not the kind of thing she'd have expected, but then again, she didn't really know him. The Ted she knew in high school was a jock. He lived and breathed football when he wasn't making some girl swoon.

She had no idea what kind of grades he got. Was he smart? She'd certainly not heard of him needing a tutor.

Why did she even care? His intelligence had nothing to do with anything. The man appeared utterly dull.

Nothing to worry about.

Fifteen minutes of the treadmill while watching the morning news, followed by a shower, and a light breakfast meant she was out the door by eight-thirty. She dropped the girls off at school and then spent the time until she had to pick them up at her lab.

She'd figured out a way to atomize the truth serum. Now, for a delivery system that wouldn't stand out or get picked up by security. Debating the merits of a lapel pin versus an umbrella handle, she quickly readied herself to leave when Mae texted. *We're done.*

Her girls set their own school hours, sometimes choosing to remain until the early evening if working on something they found interesting.

Not today.

The moment she picked them up, they started talking about their upcoming lesson with Ted. So eager. And yet all Portia wanted to do was go home, slip into some comfortable clothes, and read in bed.

However, she wasn't about to stifle their enthusiasm. The washed uniforms were in a gym bag in her trunk, alongside the satchel with their piano music books and their jazz shoes and outfits for the dance lessons she'd made them take. Her girls proved to be graceful on their feet. However, they got easily bored, claiming dance had no real practical usage. Would they think the same of martial arts?

Entering, her gaze moved right to Ted. He had a way of drawing the eye. A tall guy at over six feet, his hair had a bit of a shag to it that went well with the groomed beard he sported. The gi he wore, a two-piece outfit of loose pants and a wrap-around jacket, the fabric black unlike those of his students in white, showcased his muscular build.

It took Lin saying something she missed for Portia to realize that she stared while Ted stood behind the counter, talking to a parent. Kids warmed up on the mats, and she was glad to see she wasn't the only adult in the beginner class. They were, however, the only ones not yet dressed. Her girls walked to the locker room to change, leaving her standing with her own outfit in hand.

The parent left, and Ted eyed her. "Didn't have time to switch?"

"I came straight from work. I didn't know the girls would want to attend so soon."

"They're curious. Quite common at that age." He pointed to another door at the back. "You can use my office if you want to change. Although, I will warn, it's more of a closet." His lazy smile brought an answering one.

"Thanks."

He wasn't joking about the size of his office. He'd managed to jam a small table against one wall and had shelves bolted above it. Under the table, boxes labeled by year that she'd wager held paperwork. A thin metal stool acted as a seat. The feng shui was off the charts bad. She quickly changed so she could get out of the space.

She emerged to find everyone lined up, facing Ted. Her girls, more eager than expected, had spots in the front row. No, thanks. Portia slid to an empty place in the back.

Ted launched into a series of warm-up motions, easy enough to follow, as she pondered her mission. If she used a lapel pin, could she pack enough punch to project the truth mist at the intended target? An umbrella allowed more room to work with. However, what if it weren't raining that day? It might never make it inside.

Ted slid from exercises meant to stretch into some basic movements that proved easy and familiar. She slipped into a relaxed routine—too relaxed. When from behind, a voice murmured, "Nice form," she almost turned and decked Ted. Would have served him right for sneaking up on her. Instead, she froze mid-lunge.

"Thanks. I took a few classes when in university." Not entirely a lie. She just didn't mention the years of hand to hand she'd taken after.

"Doesn't look like you've forgotten a thing." He stepped past her, moving back to the front where he ran them through a few other drills before he clapped his hands. "Find a partner."

The students paired off, her girls against each other, and others who obviously knew each other split into twos, leaving Portia alone. She could almost predict Ted's crooked finger.

Ted gestured. "You can work with me."

"It's okay, I can watch."

"Don't be scared. I won't hurt you." He winked.

Wasn't that just like a man to think her afraid? Old Macey might have been, but Macey died a long time ago. She might have bristled a little more than necessary as she moved to stand in front of him.

Ted turned serious as he explained, "We'll go through the movements, slowly at first. Let you recognize the pattern and counter-strikes. You'll see it much like dancing in the way the motions complement each other."

"I don't dance."

His brows rose. "Is that why you said no to our date?"

He remembered asking? She dropped into a stance. Fists out. "I had a test to study for."

"The dance was a Friday night." He matched her position.

"I don't like to do things last-minute."

"Let me guess, you're the type who has lists."

"With sub-lists." She blocked his slow punch.

"I'll bet motherhood changed that."

She snorted and threw a blow of her own, which he countered. "On the contrary, I've just become even more efficient."

"That doesn't sound like much fun."

"Says a man who probably thrives on chaos."

"Actually, I like my world kept tidy." He grinned as he again threw a fist with exaggerated slowness.

She wanted to yawn. Her next blow snapped a little faster. He blocked it.

His sped up, too. "Your form really is most excellent."

"You know me, always studying. I'm a bit of a perfectionist." Try practicing almost every day for two years. Working the more scientific aspects of jobs didn't mean she wasn't trained to fight. But she couldn't exactly admit that she was a trained assassin.

"How high did you go?" He referred to the belts they used to mark progress.

"All the way."

"Then why sign up for a beginner class?"

She glanced at her twins practicing their moves, no longer bickering preteens but concentrating athletes.

"I thought it would bring us closer together."

"They think you don't know how to spar."

She shrugged. "I've learned being a parent sometimes means the occasional white lie."

"Ever take them back home?"

He referred to their hometown. The query seemed innocuous enough. "Nope. I couldn't wait to leave, and it's not as if I had anything to return to." Her parents, like the rest of the world, thought she was dead. Given her mother was abusive, and her father just plain absent, it wasn't much of a loss. Last she'd checked, they'd retired to Florida to be closer to her brother, whom they did like.

"How did you enjoy working in China?"

That was a little too knowledgeable.

How did Ted know? Lucky guess because of her girls? She faltered in her moves, and he managed to land a blow. His expression immediately turned contrite.

"Sorry about that."

"My fault." She smiled. "My turn to hit." She threw them fast and hard, forcing him to move quickly to keep up.

The concentration required stopped the questions, but the fact that he'd even asked at all was a problem. If he'd heard of her going off to study in Asia, did that mean he'd also heard about her death? Mother had done her best to scrub the internet clean about it without it being too obvious to Ronin in case he watched.

What lie could she tell that Ted would believe? None, because she couldn't take any chances, not with her daughters. She'd have to take care of Ted. Later tonight.

First, she had to take her girls home, and for once,

they were chattering. "That reminded me of yoga but with hitting," Mae remarked.

"It's more like dancing," was Lin's argument.

They fell in step when they turned their attention on Portia as they got into the car.

"We saw you sparring with Ted." The man insisted everyone use his first name, joking that he was too young to be anyone's master.

"I needed a partner."

"I think he likes you," Lin declared.

Portia cleared her throat. "We're old friends."

"Was he your *boy*friend?" Mae said with exaggeration on the *boy* part.

"No." Portia hoped neither noticed the blush in her cheeks.

"How come you've never had a boyfriend?" Mae asked.

"Because no one asked me out?" Said more as a query than a statement.

"You're pretty."

"And smart."

"Where is this coming from?" Her girls had never showed an interest in her lack of dating life before.

"Aren't you lonely?" Lin asked.

"I have you to keep me happy."

Mae frowned. "Are you still sad our father died?" The story she'd fed them when they'd become old enough to ask why they didn't have a daddy.

"Yes. Very sad." She lied because it was easier than admitting that she didn't trust men. Couldn't. Not with her past. Not with her present.

"I think you should date." Lin just wouldn't let it go.

"I'm busy."

"Don't you get tired of only working?"

Yes. The truth almost spilled from her lips. "I'm fine."

They went silent for a moment, and she thought they'd finally lost interest until Lin declared, "You need a man."

The car swerved. "I do not."

"She's right, Mother. What will you do when we leave for university? You'll be alone." Mae added her two cents.

"That's a long time away."

"Not really. Teacher says if we keep going at our current rate of education, we'll graduate by the time we're fourteen."

Four years? But they were still just children. "Maybe I'll follow you both to university. Get my masters in something."

"Mother, really. We'll have a hard enough time fitting in without you hovering," Mae said with a disdainful toss of her head.

Lin kept on with the argument. "You need someone. The book I'm reading says humans need touch to thrive."

"Guess you'll have to give me more hugs," Portia said, peeking at them in the backseat through her rearview mirror.

"Or you could get a boyfriend," Mae bluntly stated.

"Or a girlfriend, if you prefer," was Lin's addition.

They were determined to drive her insane. "I'm flattered you're both interested in my personal life. However, it is mine. Meaning the choice to date or not isn't up to you. Where is this coming from?" she asked. "Why the sudden interest in my relationship status?"

It was Mae who had a reply. "A girl in our class, her mom got a new boyfriend, and they went on a cruise."

"We can go on a cruise if you want. It doesn't require me dating."

"Don't you want to date? Or is Mae right? Do you miss our father too much?" Lin narrowed in on the cause, just not the right reason.

"Your father was special," Portia hedged. Ronin had ruined her for other men. Not only did she fear trusting, she was also afraid of letting her guard down and inviting trouble. But she couldn't tell the girls she'd been lying about their father their entire lives. Even if it was for their own good. How could she explain that he was a dangerous man who would smother and hurt them with his version of love?

Luckily, they dropped the subject by the time they reached the house. Dinner was an Alfredo sauce over grilled vegetables with garlic bread. The girls chose to watch a movie rather than do more elective homework. Although, their choice of movie—*The Godfather*—did disturb Portia, given their earlier discussion. Surely, they didn't suspect about Ronin...

Portia waited until the girls were down for the night at nine o'clock and then waited another half hour before having Joanna arrive. She lived in an apartment over the garage. Close enough to help out, without them being too much in each other's space.

"Off to work again?" Joanna chided.

"Actually, I'm going to meet a man."

That widened Joanna's eyes. "No way."

"I am." No need to mention this wasn't a date.

"Who? Do I know him?"

"The new martial arts instructor."

"The one teaching in that cruddy strip mall?" Joanna frowned. "Are you meeting him there?"

"Yes."

Joanna pursed her lips. "That's a rough place at night."

"I'll be careful."

"You'd better. You taking a gun?"

"You know I don't like firearms."

Joanna glared.

It would do no good to fight. Portia sighed and held out her hand. "Will you feel better if I borrow yours?"

"Yes." Joanna handed over the small pistol she kept tucked in her ankle holster. Portia checked to make sure the safety was engaged before sliding it into the back of her pants. She tugged her sweater over it. The addition of a jacket made it impossible to spot.

"Happy now?"

"Not really. Couldn't you meet him somewhere a little less sketchy?"

"I shouldn't be too long," was all she said, rather than curse. Why did people underestimate her?

Only once she'd gotten into her car did she call Ted. He picked up on the second ring. "Flamingo Martial Arts, Ted speaking, how can I help you?"

"Oh, thank goodness you're still there," she gushed.

"Macey? Sorry, I mean, Portia?" Flattering that he recognized her voice.

"Yes. Sorry to ring you so late. I'm sure you're eager to finish up and go home, but it wasn't until a few minutes ago as I went through my purse that I realized I couldn't find my notebook. I am hoping I dropped it in your studio. Probably in your office when I was changing?"

"Is it black with a rubber band around it?"

"Yes! You found it." She exaggerated her relief. "I need it."

"I can swing it by to you in about half an hour or so, after I'm done cleaning up here."

"That's too long. I need it to finish up some work I'm doing. I'll just run over and grab it."

"No, you shouldn't. My dojo is not in a good section of town, especially at night. I'll do my cleanup tomorrow and bring it now if it's urgent."

Just like Joanna, he thought her too weak to handle herself. "No, you will most certainly not. I'm a big girl, and you shouldn't be going out of your way. I'll be by in about ten minutes to grab it. I'll park right out front if that makes you feel better."

"Not really."

"I'll keep my doors locked until the very last second."

The remark brought a snort. "As if that would stop anyone. You're too pretty to be roaming my area at night."

The compliment brought unexpected pleasure. But rather than accept it, she tossed it back to him. "I could say the same of you."

He sighed. "No one is interested in selling me on the black market."

"I wouldn't be so certain. I'm sure a few of your organs are harvestable." A tart reply, to which he laughed.

"Anyone ever tell you you're stubborn?"

"All the time. Usually before they agree to what I want." Because Portia wasn't a pushover anymore.

"Let me bring it to you. Please. It would make me feel better."

"Too late. I'm already halfway there. See you soon." Before he could argue, she hung up and simmered over his remark. As if she was too dainty to handle going out on her own.

Why couldn't she be smart and dangerous? And why did she care what he thought? Soon, he'd realize just how much he underestimated her, but by then, it would be too late for him.

She raced down the road and parked across from the strip of stores, noting it was pretty quiet this time of night, with only a handful of vehicles scattered up and down the street. The light shining from the window of his studio meant she could see inside where Ted moved back and forth, wiping down the mats with a long-handled mop.

He turned as she stepped out of the car, set his mop aside, and headed for the door, pulling her notebook off the counter as he approached. He truly wasn't keen on having her stick around. So much for the girls' theory that he crushed on her.

Portia opened the door and stepped in. "Hi, thank goodness you found my book."

He held it out. "Here you go."

"Thanks." She tucked it into her purse, but she didn't

immediately go. "Listen, Ted, about our past... I'd really prefer it if you didn't say anything in front of my girls, or talk about it at all, to anyone, actually."

"Hiding from something?"

"No. What makes you say that?" She kept her hand in her purse, fingers wrapped around a syringe.

"Come on, Macey. Portia. Whatever name you want to use. I'm not stupid. According to some news report, you died in an accident while in China."

She went numb inside. "I don't know what you're talking about."

"Someone did a good job of scrubbing the articles."

Her blood ran cold. He'd been looking her up. How? How had Marie not spotted this during their electronic surveillance? "That was a long time ago."

"Does anyone know you're alive?"

"No. And I'd prefer to keep it that way." She pulled out her hand, tucked into her sleeve, hiding the needle she'd slipped into her bag before leaving the house. She'd only get one shot. "Haven't you ever wanted to start over?"

"Yeah. I guess you could call this my do-over project." He swept a hand around the dojo.

"Well, consider Portia Stalone my do-over, which is why you can't tell anyone about me."

A grave expression creased his face. "Are you in danger?"

Every minute of every hour, if Ronin ever found out that she lived. She shook her head. "Just trying to get away from my past. So, I'd appreciate it if you could keep quiet."

"Will do. But I will say, if you are in trouble—"

She cut him off. "I'm fine. Thanks. I'd better go and get my work done. It was nice seeing you again." She went to hug him, which would get her close enough to use the syringe, only the bells over his door jangled.

"Oh, shit," Ted muttered as he shoved her behind him. She might have protested, but chose instead to observe why he suddenly appeared so tense.

A trio of men walked in. Gang toughs by the swagger, she'd wager. But it was the one in the middle that caused her to pause.

A man who should be dead. An old acquaintance who would probably recognize her. She tucked closer behind Ted, using his body as a shield, hoping the man had not gotten a good look at her face.

Then she prayed to a deity that didn't listen.

CHAPTER FOUR

FUCK ME. Ted didn't have to glance behind to realize Portia had stiffened, probably in fear. Just his shit luck, Taotie would show before she had a chance to leave.

"You're early." Ted tried to draw the thug's attention to him.

"Am I early or just in time? Who's that hiding behind you? I wasn't aware you had a girlfriend. You seem more the type to be best friends with your hand." Taotie's gaze strayed past Ted.

"She's no one," Ted quickly said, not liking Taotie's interest. Worse, though, he could sense Portia's coiled tension. He had no way to reassure her that Taotie wouldn't touch her. Just scare her a bit to make himself look big. Or so Ted hoped.

"No one?" Taotie repeated in a mocking tone. "Is that any way to talk about your lady friend?"

"She's a customer and was just about to leave."

"She stays," Taotie stated.

"Why? She has nothing to do with our business."

"Everything that happens in this neighborhood is my business." Taotie shifted to his left, and Ted almost moved to match him, only he knew it would just make things worse. For some reason, Taotie was determined to force Portia out of hiding.

And he discovered why a moment later when Portia stepped out of his shadow to say, "Hello, Chen."

"Shit," he muttered. Didn't take a genius to see that they knew each other and had not parted on good terms. Was Taotie the father of her children? That didn't seem right. She was much too smart to have hooked up with a low-class thug.

"Well, well. It is you. Macey Munroe." Taotie cocked his head. "You almost fooled me with the hair. And your face. Have you gained weight?"

"I would ask the same of you," was her cool reply.

"It's been a while."

"Not long enough." The tight control in her voice was the only thing that betrayed her angst.

Taotie wore a different tracksuit than the previous night, but the smirk held the exact same arrogance. "My lucky day."

"Who is this?" Ralph asked, confused by the exchange. Then again, Ted would wager it didn't take much to muddle him.

"A dead woman. Who is not very dead, as it turns out. Tell me, Macey, were you even on that helicopter when it crashed?" Taotie queried.

"What do you think?" Macey didn't cower before Taotie. Brave even as it was stupid. The thug wasn't one to tolerate what he considered to be disrespect.

Taotie's expression hardened. "You fucking cunt. You tried to kill me."

"Me? I wasn't the one with the gun."

Ted blinked. What the fuck was happening?

"Holy fuck, is this the broad you were telling us about? The one that got you kicked out of China?" Ralph's gaze went wide.

"This cunt conspired with a bitch to kill me and escape," Taotie confirmed.

"Actually, I had nothing to do with what happened. But can't say as I minded either," Macey declared.

"Because of you, I almost died." Taotie's face twisted with rage.

"Oops." She offered a non-apologetic shrug. "Unfortunately, a necessary thing given you wouldn't have stepped aside so I could escape."

"The whole reason I was placed as your guard was because Ronin knew you were thinking of running."

Ronin. Ted stored the named for later. The unfolding drama couldn't be missed.

"Can you blame me? He treated me no better than a prisoner."

"Living in the lap of luxury," Taotie spat.

"Luxury?" Rather than show meekness, Macey's chin lifted. "He bought me clothes to hide the bruises he left. Showered me in jewels as if that was supposed to make me forgive his abuse."

The hands by Ted's sides tightened. It was getting harder and harder to listen.

"Whine, whine, bitch, bitch," Taotie mocked. "Such a hard life. He would have given you everything. But then you supposedly died in that crash, and Ronin went ballistic. Guess who was left behind to deal with it? He blamed me for everything. I was the one who got the brunt of his punishment."

"Couldn't have been that bad, given you look fine," was her tart reply.

Ted could have winced. Talking back wouldn't help the situation.

"Fine?" Taotie barked. "I was shot in the head!" He shoved back the thick hank of hair that usually covered his forehead, showing a puckered mark.

"A little bit too much to the left, judging by the scar. I can't believe she missed." Macey shook her head. "She's not usually so careless."

Ted blinked. She didn't just say that.

She did. And wasn't done. "Guess you had more empty space rattling around inside that fat head than anyone would have imagined."

Ted almost took a step back. Why did she deliberately antagonize?

To his surprise, Taotie didn't fly into a rage, but with a wave of his hand, his friends fanned out. The man smiled, and a knife slipped into his palm. "The doctors claim I am a living miracle."

"Have to say I'm surprised to see you alive. Ronin doesn't usually tolerate failure." She seemed determined to make Taotie snap.

He'd never heard of this Ronin guy, but if she was willing to pretend to be dead, it couldn't be good.

Taotie's hands curled into fists. "I suffered his displeasure. For the first two weeks, I was in the hospital.

Ronin came by every day just so he could tell me I should have died instead of you."

"Why didn't he kill you?" She sounded almost curious.

"Because he wanted me to suffer. Because of you," Taotie spat, "I spent months in a hospital, a dirty one because Ronin wanted me to hurt. Whenever I got close to healing, he'd send someone to beat me up. The only way I got it to stop was by escaping China. Starting over. I had to claw my way back up, and even then, only made it as far as running a two-bit operation in America."

"You should aim for higher in life. Maybe, I don't know, try getting a real job that doesn't involve breaking any laws or helping an asshole hold a woman prisoner." Macey just wouldn't stop.

Ted didn't know if he should admire her or ask if she'd forgotten to take some meds.

"Fuck you," Taotie spat.

"I see your vocabulary hasn't improved much." She shook her head.

"Let's see how well you talk once I'm done with you."

"You won't be hurting me." A statement that only served to confuse Ted. She seemed way too calm.

"You're right, I won't. But I have a feeling I know someone who will. Wait until Ronin hears you're alive. Maybe returning you will appease him."

"I am not going back, and you won't be telling him anything." Macey stepped closer to Taotie, hands tucked behind her back. Ted noticed that she had a needle in her hand.

Hold on, why did she have a needle?

"Bitch, you keep talking like you have a choice. In case you didn't notice, I'm the one holding all the cards." Taotie gestured to his posse. "Once I return you, I won't have to stoop to working shit jobs with morons."

"Hey!" Ralph protested.

"Shut the fuck up. I wasn't talking about you." Taotie's gaze slid to the newest member, who scowled.

"You better not be calling me dumb," asserted the dumb third wheel.

Ralph rolled his eyes and cuffed the guy. "Shut up."

While they bickered, Macey's hand with the syringe dropped to her side. She palmed it as if to hide it. What did it contain? She was a doctor. Perhaps some kind of sedative, her equivalent of a pepper spray for protection? *Please don't let it be something contagious that burns the skin.*

"You really should have made better choices, Chen. Unfortunate that you never learned, because now I'm going to have to act when I'd rather not." She shook her head, almost sadly.

"What are you going to do? Call the cops? Go ahead. They won't touch me," Taotie taunted.

The truth. Ted couldn't help but feel sorry for Macey. A woman who'd escaped her abuser only to have a fluke of fate have her run into someone that would notify this Ronin fellow. This wouldn't end well for Macey.

Unless he stepped in.

Usually, he stayed out of conflicts. Especially when violence might occur. It was all too easy to succumb to the adrenaline and react with deadly force. Harder to deal with the consequences.

Standing up to Chen and his minions would result in him losing his business, maybe even his life. Blackmailing thugs couldn't allow anyone to question their power.

But not acting put Macey in danger.

Damn the rusty hero inside him that creaked to life. "Leave Macey alone. Pretend you never saw her," Ted said, finally interrupting their verbal duel.

"Don't get involved," Macey stated.

"I'd rather not, trust me, but I'm also not the kind of asshole who can stand by and let him take a woman by force. It ain't right." It was one thing for Taotie to threaten Ted. It bothered him seeing it directed at someone else.

"Chen is my problem, not yours."

"Listen to the cunt. This doesn't concern you. Stay out of it." Taotie eyed him briefly, his gaze flat and deadly. A man motivated by greed.

"How much to keep her safe?" Ted asked, mentally tallying how much he could afford.

"More than you can pay," Taotie declared. "Speaking of paying..." He eyed Ralph. "Mustn't forget to collect. Handle him while I take care of the woman."

Ralph cracked his knuckles. "You heard the boss. Time to pay up, karate man."

"It's not karate," Ted muttered.

"You can call it whatever the fuck you like, I don't care. So long as you pay the money you owe us," Taotie snapped. "Now, get the cash and hand it over before I get really pissed and put you in a cast."

"Move." Ralph shoved Ted, but he planted his feet and rocked with the blow.

He had his eye on Taotie, who'd grabbed Macey's arm, snapping, "Let's go."

She glanced at the hand on her body. Having seen her ability to defend during his class, he knew she was capable of throwing it off, but she didn't remove it.

Was she afraid to fight? Now wasn't the time. Going with the thugs wouldn't end well for her. Ted ignored Ralph and said in a low growl, "Leave her alone."

She peeked at him. Expression calm. *Too* calm. "It's okay, Ted. I can handle Chen and his friend."

"That's what she thinks," guffawed the third dummy with a grab of his crotch that earned him a slap from Taotie.

"No touching her. Not until I talk to Ronin and see what he wants to do."

"Who is this fucker, Ronin? And why are you so eager to suck his dick?" muttered dummie, earning himself another slap.

"Let's go get the dough." Ralph prodded Ted.

Ted glanced at Macey, who'd tucked a hand into her purse. Where was the panic? What had she done with that needle?

"It's in the back," Ted lied as he moved towards his office, hating that he appeared the coward in front of Macey. However, he knew three against one wasn't the type of odds he wanted to attempt. Not when he could rid himself of one problem right now.

He waited until Ralph had cleared the door to his office before he moved, yanking Ralph close, wrapping an arm around the man's throat and kicking the back of his knee, bringing him to the floor. The chunky guy struggled and sought to get out of Ted's grip. And failed, because sometimes size didn't mean shit. It was all in the technique.

It took longer than Ted liked before Ralph stopped twitching. Ted held on for an extra moment before pulling some belts from his drawer. He trussed the unconscious fellow quickly, hand to foot, then crept to the partially ajar door and listened.

He heard nothing. Had they already left?

He pushed the door open enough to peek through, wondering if Taotie or his third had remained behind. The dojo appeared empty. Ted stepped fully out and crossed the room, his bare feet silent on the mat, aware his body was illuminated to anyone outside looking through the window, making him an excellent target.

The glass didn't shatter with a bullet, and he could have cursed as the bell tinkled when he opened the door. He needn't have worried.

Nothing moved on the sidewalk. He looked left and right, noticing the other stores closed already for the night except for the everything mart on the corner which sold cigarettes, booze, condoms, and snack food. Everything you needed to live.

He saw no one, heard nothing. Yet he doubted they'd gone far. He scanned the parked cars, three in clearly marked spots, the one right across from his dojo the kind of SUV he could see Macey driving. Not one of them had lights on, or an engine running. None were the familiar Honda Civic he was used to seeing Taotie drive. Had they left? He'd assumed they'd wait for Ralph.

If they had, then that meant they'd parked out of sight because he highly doubted they'd walked. Before he could head for the alley running behind the strip mall, the next most logical choice, he heard a bang. Gunshot! Before the second was done echoing, he was sprinting.

The alley lining the length of the strip mall had less light, but he didn't need much to see the car parked, a sleek Civic, low to the ground, black body trimmed in subtle hints of emerald green. And slamming its trunk shut? Macey.

She whirled and leaned against it and exclaimed when she saw him. "Ted. Are you okay?"

"Yeah. Are you? Where's Taotie?" He searched the grungy alley with its dumpster reeking of rancid garbage but saw no one.

A guarded expression fell over her features. "That pretentious prick and his sidekick are rethinking their choices in life."

"Where are they?"

She didn't reply. His gaze went to the trunk.

Surely, his assumption proved wrong. "Did you kill them?"

"Do you really think I'm capable of that?" A non-answer. And he might have said never if this were the old Macey he'd admired from afar in high school. Yet the woman in front of him wasn't the girl he used to know.

This woman oozed cool confidence.

What had she done?

Ted stepped closer, "What's going on, Macey?"

She sighed. "I really wished I hadn't run into you, Ted. You didn't deserve to get caught up in this."

"Caught up in what? Let me help you." She was in trouble, and while not a man prone to ride any proverbial white horses, he couldn't help but want to come to her aid.

"You can't help me."

"You don't know that."

"Actually, I do know. You don't want to get involved, trust me." Her lips turned down.

"You're really scared of this Ronin guy, aren't you?"

"He's a bad man."

"And the twins' father," he stated.

She nodded.

"He doesn't know you and the girls are alive." He wanted to get the story straight.

"He thinks we're dead, and I'd prefer it stayed that way. Now, if we're done..." She pushed away from the car.

"I can help you hide," he offered.

"Why do you keep assuming I need aid? I've been taking care of myself just fine up until now." Her gaze met his, glinting with annoyance.

"That was before you messed with the Evening Swords, the gang that runs this neighborhood. You'll need an ally."

She snorted. "I'll be long gone before they find out what happened to their street rats."

"What are you planning to do?"

"Better if you don't know. Better if you don't ask. You never know what you're capable of until pushed to your limits." He only recognized her haunted expression because he'd seen it so many times in the mirror. The resigned face that said: *"I've seen and done shit you can't understand."*

"Is this your way of saying you're going to try and kill me, too?"

"I'm not going to kill you." She stepped away from the car, close enough to him that she had to tilt her head back to look him in the eye. "I'm sorry," she whispered.

"Why?"

Rather than reply, she leaned up and brushed her mouth over his. A surprise. "Sorry because you can't be allowed to remember." The needle from before finally made its appearance, jabbing into his side. He reeled away from her and yanked it from his skin. Too late. The contents had been emptied.

He frowned. "What did you do?" She worked in a lab, had she injected him with the bubonic plague?

"Just a sedative so you'll stop talking." She grabbed his hand and held him in place.

"I can't sleep. I have to—" His thoughts were sluggish, meaning he blinked a few times as she poked the back of his hand with a second needle.

"Wass dat?" he slurred.

"Something to make sure you forget."

CHAPTER FIVE

PORTIA BARELY MANAGED to grab Ted when he slumped. Given his size, she couldn't do more than make sure he didn't slam his face off the pavement. The rest of him, though...it crumpled in a limp heap because she'd sedated his ass. She had to. The reasons were too many to count. Talk about the worst freaking luck in the world. Running into Chen, of all people.

How? What were the chances? She'd lived here for years and never suspected that one of her biggest enemies might be nearby. She hated the man and had roundly cursed—after she'd gotten over her panic—when she found out that he'd lived after getting shot in the head.

Chen didn't deserve the privilege of living. The man was utter scum. Not bad enough that he'd kept her prisoner, he used to gloat about it, too—saying the nastiest things. Detail what he'd do to her body when Ronin tired of her being his wife. If Ronin ever heard, he'd have gutted Chen himself. But the bastard never uttered his threats anywhere near the cameras watching or the microphones listening. A clever feat given how many of them there were.

So many eyes and ears spying on her. Once she became aware of Ronin's penchant for voyeurism, she'd learned to notice their presence.

They were everywhere.

But Chen knew a few spots where he could speak freely. And to add insult, Chen was also the one person Ronin never questioned. When she complained about him, Ronin would get that dark look in his eyes. The one that reminded her to tread carefully. *"He would never betray me."*

Given their bond, she had no doubt Chen would have done anything to regain Ronin's approval. He'd have called Ronin and announced his discovery the moment he had her secured. If she'd not acted, Ronin would have found out that she was still alive. Would have learned about the twins. That couldn't happen.

Chen had to die.

The thought hit her inside the dojo, the second she recognized Chen. The question was, how would she kill him? Unlike some of the other moms, Portia didn't often have hands-on missions. They preferred her coming up with interesting solutions in her lab. Recipes with unique delivery systems to fake accidents. Pricey accidents, and only if the target proved worthy.

Killer Moms discriminated when it came to clients. And given their success rate, people paid. That money kept Portia and the girls safe. But earning it meant letting go of some of her morals.

The younger kid, Eddie as Chen called him, walked

ahead with a lanky slouch, his pants sagging in the ass. Would it kill him to get the right size or wear a belt? So unattractive. And stupid, too. She could see why Chen called him a fucktwat.

Chen had not really changed much. His hair was longer and hung over his forehead, and his face had a few lines in it, but he retained the same arrogance as always as he strutted beside her. He oozed smugness, certain that he had her beat. After all, Macey was just a woman. Harmless. Meek.

I'm not Macey. I'm Portia.

Portia never ducked her head, never promised subservience. Never took shit. Not anymore. She made her own choices, and she knew how to stop people who would hurt her.

She'd killed worse than Chen, but she'd have to tackle it right if she wanted to escape clean. Portia allowed Chen to keep his grip around her upper arm and followed his quick march that led her around the building.

The kid held up a key fob, and lights flashed on a car parked in the alley. A rather dark back street where pavement met garbage. Bags dumped beside dumpsters overflowing, mostly because there were those who went through it in search of treasures.

No cameras appeared to videotape, and yet she had no doubt that someone might be watching. Many of the businesses along this stretch might be closed for the night, their metal doors leading to the alley locked tight, but she'd wager there were some who lived on the second floors. Some had their windows lit, creating a glow on the other side of closed blinds. Through one lacking a covering, she could see the flashing lights of images playing on a screen. Too much noise might draw one of the inhabitants to a window for a peek.

She'd have to act quietly. A pity she didn't have enough syringes in her purse to knock everyone out. As it stood, she had one sleep and one memory wipe. She already had plans for their use.

At the small of her back, concealed under her jacket, she carried a small revolver. Lacking any kind of stamp identifying the maker, it also lacked a serial number. The grip of it didn't hold DNA or prints very well. A good disposable weapon. Only the best for Aunt Joanna. She was kind of glad she'd agree to take it with her now.

It was an insult and a boon that Chen never thought to frisk her. In his mind, Macey didn't carry weapons. Macey would just blithely go along.

I'm not Macey.

She'd never been happier about the choice to become someone else.

She didn't draw the gun, not yet. The element of surprise would be key because firing it would draw attention, maybe even the police. It would remain tucked away until the last second. Maybe she'd get lucky and get away with using only her wits and fists to subdue them.

"Want me to use the rope or the cuffs?" Eddie asked, popping the trunk. The casual nature of the query let her know this happened often enough that he thought nothing of it. Chen hadn't changed one bit.

"Not much point in either. She's not going to do anything. She never does." Chen smirked.

"Are you sure about that?" She couldn't help but taunt

him. "After all, didn't you accuse me of conspiring to kill and escape you?" She smiled.

"You fucking cunt. You will pay for that." Chen's fingers bruised as he dragged her to a stop by the gaping trunk.

Better-sized than expected. A good thing it wasn't the big fellow out here with them. He'd be a little harder to stuff in there.

But two skinny guys? The trunk would do just fine.

Chen shoved her towards Eddie, spitting. "You know what, get the rope. And the gag. Someone needs a lesson in obeying her betters."

I'll show him who's better.

She caught the edge of the trunk as Eddie chuckled. "I'll truss her ass tighter than a turkey at Thanksgiving."

Ignoring Portia, Eddie leaned into the trunk. Gave her his back!

It was insulting how little regard they both had for her. At the same time, she'd never get a better chance.

Portia dove forward and slammed the trunk down, catching Eddie hard enough that he yelled. When the lid bounced up, she ducked, heaved Eddie's legs, and dumped him into the opening.

The trunk slammed down in time for her to whirl and catch Chen's surprised expression.

"What the fuck?"

She leaned against the bouncing car as Eddie thrashed in the enclosed space. "Did you really think I was going to just let you waltz me back to Ronin?"

"I don't care how you go. I'll drag you with all your limbs broken if need be." He cracked his knuckles.

If he meant to frighten, he failed miserably. She straightened. "Only one of us is walking away today. And it is my pleasure to inform you that it won't be you."

"I am going to break you, fucking cunt!" Chen finally snapped. He dove at her, and she ducked, using her head and shoulder to block him, ramming hard into his stomach. The air oomphed from his lungs. He wheezed, trying to suck in a breath, which was when she projected straight up, the top of her head slamming into his chin. His jaw snapped shut, but he screamed nonetheless. Possibly bit his tongue.

Ouch. She didn't actually feel any sympathy for him, not when her girls' lives were on the line. Cold. Methodical. This was a problem that had to be solved.

Eddie thumped against the inside of the trunk. She grabbed Chen's head before she popped it open. Chen's face came down, and the pair rammed together. The blow sent Chen wailing to his knees. She ignored him as Eddie attempted to emerge, rising with a yell of rage. She throat-punched him.

A lethal move.

While he clawed at his crushed larynx, she focused on Chen. He'd finally fumbled for the knife he kept tucked in his pocket. Still with the switchblade. She recollected the adept way he used to wield it, an extension of himself that he liked to use to carve people into strips. Toying with them. She could only assume he killed them since she never saw those folks again.

He enjoyed hurting. How would he feel having the roles reversed? She would have loved to show him how that felt. He'd been one of those to hurt her. But that *smacked more of revenge rather than protection. The safety of the twins came first and foremost. Now that she was compromised, every second counted. She had to deal with the situation and then get the girls out of here.*

Hand to hand with Chen when he had a knife? Time to even the odds and risk attention.

The gun emerged, and she placed the first bullet in Chen's head. Then another for good measure—this had been done before, after all. Just like a zombie, he wouldn't rise again. He fell face-first into the trunk on top of a frantic-eyed Eddie, who would have hurt her badly if given a chance. Another person who didn't deserve to live.

She felt nothing as she fired again. She'd just finished tipping Chen into the trunk and closing it when Ted came looking.

He should have stayed inside his dojo.

Now he drooled on the pavement.

She rubbed her forehead and paced. "This is not good," she muttered. She glanced at the windows and didn't see any faces pressed against the glass, but that didn't mean no one watched—or recorded. Even now, video might be uploaded to the internet.

What a mess. She pulled her phone and made her first call to Aunt Joanna.

"Hey, Auntie, how are the girls?" Code for: *Is it safe to talk?*

"Sleeping like bears in winter," the reply for: *Go ahead.*

Portia slumped against the car. "You might have been right about me staying away from this part of town."

"What happened?"

"Let's just say I am going to need a cleanup crew for at least a double."

"Shit. That bad? What happened?"

"I ran into Ronin's ex-right-hand man."

No need to say who, Joanna was well aware of Portia's history. "Oh, fuck. Chen is in town?"

"Was." She eyed the trunk. "He won't pose a threat anymore."

"Good."

"Not really. He wasn't alone." Which made her wonder about the third guy. Still inside the dojo? Eyeing Ted on the ground, she had to wonder since he'd emerged into the alley alone.

"Have you neutralized all the threats."

"Two permanently, one...kind of. The fourth is pending."

"Four? I thought you said it was a double."

"So far for cleanup." She eyed Ted. "That number could go up."

"Geezus, girl. I warned you about that neighborhood," Joanna barked. "I'm coming."

"You will do no such thing," Portia huffed. "You need to stay at the house and guard the girls. Get ready to leave."

"I thought you stopped the threat."

"I did. I don't think Chen had a chance to say anything to anyone, but I can't take the chance that *he* might find out." There was only one *he*.

"Given you've only neutralized two of the problems, maybe instead of yapping at me, you should be handling the other two," Joanna chided, but Portia knew it came from a place of love, the brusque kind that was frightened and frustrated because Joanna couldn't be there to help.

"I'm going. wanted you to be aware of what happened before I went hunting for Chen's other man."

"And the fourth one?"

She eyed Ted on the ground. The right answer would be to get rid of all the witnesses to her sudden return to the living. Meaning Ted should die. And yet, she couldn't do it. He'd done nothing wrong. She'd given him the serum, meaning he'd wake up and not remember anything from the past few days. Just long enough for him to forget that he'd seen her again.

"Don't worry about Ted. He's just a martial arts instructor. A nobody. I've made sure he'll forget."

"He's a loose end."

"You can't dispose of him. He's—" She'd have to give the right excuse if she hoped to keep him from being a casualty in this nasty situation. "Ted is my boyfriend."

Dead silence.

Then laughter. "Bullshit," Joanna exclaimed. "You just met the guy like yesterday. The girls told me about him."

"Did they mention that we knew each other in high school?" She winced in anticipation.

"Portia!" Joanna yelled. "How long have you been compromised?"

Walking away from the car towards the end of the alley, she tried to calm Joanna. "It's fine. I knew Ted before everything happened with Ronin."

"Doesn't matter, you know links to your past aren't allowed," she exclaimed. "Does Mother know?"

"Yeah." And given the newest situation, Mother—real name Marie—wouldn't hesitate to act. Which was why she needed to cement things a bit further. She needed to keep Ted safe. He shouldn't have to pay for her mistakes. "I didn't tell her we were involved romantically." She glanced back at Ted. The things she had to say to keep him alive.

"Do you love him?"

The word almost caused her to erupt into a coughing fit. Pausing at the alley entrance, Portia leaned against the brick wall and stared at the sky. "Does it matter?" she asked, even as she knew the answer. Any tie to her past had to be severed.

"You know you can't stay." Even with Chen disposed of, the risk of someone else from her past being around remained high. After all, there had been two in less than a week. How many more familiar faces would she run into? But at the same time, where would she go?

"I can't just move in the middle of the night. How would I explain it to the girls?"

"We'll figure something out. Get home as soon as you can. I'll have a cleaning crew sent asap."

Portia hung up and sighed. What a mess.

Which meant, it had to get worse.

CHAPTER SIX

"WHAT THE FUCK ARE YOU DOING?" The expletive had her looking up and seeing the chunky fellow from inside. "Where is the boss?"

"He's in the car."

Chunk eyed her, and then his gaze moved past to the body lying in the alley. His eyes widened. "What happened?"

"I can explain," she said softly, stepping towards him, wishing she'd not tossed the gun into the trunk. But she'd wanted it cleaned with the bodies.

Chunk retreated. "Stay away."

"Do you really think I could hurt anyone?" She batted her lashes and did her best to look innocent.

Failed miserably given he made a sign against evil, then turned and ran.

Seriously? She couldn't let him escape. He'd heard too much. Wasting precious seconds retrieving the gun, Portia shoved it into her purse before she chased him.

The guy zig-zagged and ran pretty quick for someone

his size, which with his head start, proved enough to keep him out of reach. He was obviously no stranger to escape attempts.

Chunk darted into a restaurant, the bold sign in the windows offering fresh eggrolls that smelled divine and tickled her taste buds as she followed him inside. She tucked her hand into her purse, fingers questing for the gun.

The bell over the door jangled, and she halted as the eyes of more than a few patrons chose to peruse Portia. None of them moved from their seat, so she remained still and cast her gaze around. The big fellow had disappeared, probably into the back. Through the kitchen because he knew this neighborhood, and she didn't.

Rather than waste her time following, she should be readying herself to leave.

Permanently.

Ugh. She did not want to explain a sudden move to the girls.

Emerging from the restaurant, she quickly stomped back to the dojo, eyeing her car parked across the street and debating if she should just jump in and go. She didn't have time to waste. Even now, Chunk might be finding a way to get ahold of Ronin.

But she couldn't just leave Ted in the alley. Not with a cleanup crew coming. They might not realize that she didn't want him dead.

How would she carry him? She'd need help for sure. She'd figure it out once she—

"Where the hell is he?" She turned into the alley to find Ted's body gone. She might have thought herself in the wrong place, yet the car remained. The smelly dumpster, too. But no handsome dude dressed in black pajamas, passed out like a sleeping prince.

Had he gotten up and walked away? Doubtful. She'd given him a proper dose of sedative for a man his size.

How then did his body disappear?

Wee-oo. Wee-oo.

The distant wail of sirens might be only a coincidence. Or someone called the cops because they'd heard the gunshots. She couldn't take any chances. She had to leave. Now.

She practically ran for her car. The noise from the sirens would rouse residents, lured by the possible violence and crime. She might have been seen. Dammit. She sped away from the neighborhood, watching the rearview a little too much. Waiting for signs of flashing lights that would mean a change in plans.

No one chased her, and she made it home with no problem, pulling right into the garage and sealing it shut. The car was compromised, meaning they'd leave in the minivan. The moment she rolled out of her vehicle, she worked on the plates. They'd need a clean getaway, which meant adopting a new name and address. To muddle things further, a touch of a button inside the wheel well ionized the frame, and the color shifted, going from white to blue. It wasn't an evenly applied blue, and there were hints of white still in places where it failed to switch, but at night, no one would notice the oddness of it. They just needed it long enough to get to their next ride.

Then she'd set it on fire.

Joanna held the door open to the kitchen. "You're home sooner than expected. I didn't think they'd get a crew out there so quick."

"I had to leave before they arrived. Cops were coming."

Joanna arched a brow. "And you ran away?"

"I don't have time to be arrested."

"For your information, they weren't coming for you. Had you popped into their frequency, or called me, I could have told you. They were answering a domestic."

The reminder had her glancing at her watch. She'd never even thought to use the monitoring police band feature. "Because, of course, you were monitoring the area. Because you don't think I can handle myself." Just like Chen, Joanna sometimes underestimated her. Despite knowing her irritation was with herself, she snapped at her friend.

"Don't get your panties in a twist. Of course, I was watching and listening. I started the moment you walked out that door. You told me to guard those girls, and that means being aware of every possible danger, including their mother going to a known bad neighborhood. What if they'd carjacked you? Or decided you were an easy mark for human trafficking?"

"I went armed."

"A good thing, but I'll remind you that this wouldn't have been an issue if you'd stayed home in the first place."

"You were right. Okay?" Portia hugged her. "We need to make preparations to leave. If the cleanup crew doesn't get there soon, then it might not be long before someone discovers Chen and his buddy in that car."

"Even if they do find the bodies, no one will immediately make a connection between his death and you."

"I don't want to take any chances."

A beep had Joanna holding up her phone. "No need to panic. The car and the bodies have been removed."

"Oh, thank goodness." One worry resolved.

"And Tanya is monitoring online for any social media videos or images being posted." The KM hacker would wipe anything she came across.

"Did the crew see Ted?"

"Where did you leave him?"

"He was on the ground until I chased Chunk. Then he was gone." Maybe he'd recovered from the sedative and staggered back to the dojo.

"And she tells me this now?" Joanna growled as she typed into her phone.

Beep. "No sign of your boyfriend."

Portia winced. The lie seemed stupid now.

Beep. "Hmm." Joanna glanced at the screen then moved for the coffee pot. Indicating that she expected a long night ahead.

"What's *hmm* supposed to mean?"

"Nothing."

"Joanna!" Portia growled her name.

"Don't get pissy. The cleanup crew might have set fire to the martial arts place."

"What? That's insane. Why would they burn it down?"

"Mother's orders."

"Mother knows?"

Joanna rolled her eyes. "She knows everything."

"How? I haven't called her." Portia's gaze narrowed. "You told her I went to see Ted. You knew about him."

"Don't get that look with me. You know what my job is."

"Your job isn't to make my life more difficult."

"No, but it *is* to make sure you and the girls are safe. The moment your cover was compromised, Marie called me. She wanted me ready to move with the twins if needed."

Just one of the many backup plans in case Portia was ever found. "I'm so tired of living on the edge of a sword."

"One day, we'll find a way to get to the bastard."

Doubtful. It seemed as if the evilest in the world were often the most untouchable. Impossible to get near without in-depth vetting. Poisoning impossible unless willing to take the chance that others would die, too because the most paranoid didn't always eat from the plate set in front of them.

The truly evil ones had deals with the devil because they had the best damned luck when it came to avoiding ambush.

Would Ted have the kind of luck that didn't have him roasting to a crisp? This was all her fault. Ted was probably dead because he'd recognized her. Portia rubbed the throbbing spot between her eyes. When would this end?

Beep. Joanna glanced at her phone. "Marie wants you to call her."

"I will. I just need to check on the girls first." Needed to reassure herself that they were safe for the moment.

"They're fine."

"I'm not," was Portia's mutter as she stalked from the kitchen. Tonight, she'd been as bad as those she killed. She'd done it without remorse. She should feel guilt, and yet as she gazed upon the sweet faces of her daughters, she knew one thing for sure. *I'd do it again.*

She'd kill as many times as it took to keep her sweet angels safe. Had been doing things she never thought herself capable of since having them. She placed a soft kiss on each forehead. Let them sleep a few minutes longer. Who knew how long before they'd get their next rest.

In her bedroom, she pulled out a carry-on-sized suitcase, already partially packed. Phone tucked between her shoulder and her ear, she added toiletries to it as she rang Marie.

"I told you we should have gotten rid of him," Marie said in lieu of hello.

"Who, Chen? Yeah, you should have."

"Don't you dare start. I'm talking about your old school chum. I told you he would be trouble."

"It wasn't Ted's fault that he was getting shaken down by Chen. I still can't believe the guy survived."

"You and me both. Next time, I'll make sure I take his head clean off."

"There won't be a next time." She quickly told Marie what had happened since Joanna had only managed to feed her part of the story.

At the end of it, Marie cursed in French. "*Maudit!* This is not good. The man that went missing will probably contact Ronin." Anyone looking for a payout would because Portia would wager that he'd pay dearly for news of her whereabouts.

"I know. I'm packing a few things and then grabbing the girls and Joanna."

"To go where? I don't have a new identity set up for you yet." Creating a persona that could withstand scrutiny took time.

"I can't stay here." Not with the fear that Ronin could descend at any second. Never mind that she already knew he was still in China. Her phone was programmed to advise her anytime he moved. He was the bogeyman who could appear at will, especially in her nightmares. "I have an emergency set of papers I can use for now."

"What about visiting one of your sisters?" Marie suggested.

Meaning another Killer Mom. "No. I won't put them in danger."

"Then where? A motel on the side of the road?" Marie snapped, and it wasn't out of anger at Portia. Knowing her as Portia did, she knew it rose from a feeling of helplessness. Marie didn't like letting her girls down, and she'd take this sudden move as a failure on her part.

"I was thinking of maybe visiting a beach." Portia hadn't actually thought further ahead than jumping into the van and driving until she could drive no more.

"Beach? That's a great idea," Marie declared. "You need to go on a cruise."

"Are you insane? This is not the time for a vacation."

"But what better way to hide than on a boat full of strangers. Not to mention, the girls won't think to question."

A sudden vacation in the middle of school? They would question and argue. Yet it was just the type of thing that might work. Besides, the girls *had* just brought it up the other day. Still...

"We can't sail around forever."

"A week should do it. Give me enough time to close down your life where you are and have a new one ready to go."

"I'll need to bring Joanna." Two eyes watching were better than one.

"Of course. Give me an hour or so, and I'll get a flight and itinerary set up."

"Sounds good. I'll wake the girls and get to the airport." She had a second set of passports for them all. The only problem was, she couldn't let the girls question their change in name. She'd handle it on the ride to the terminal.

Marie sighed. "I'm sorry, Portia. I know you were hoping you wouldn't have to leave."

"It's not your fault." It was hers for not uprooting the moment she ran into Ted.

Hanging up with Marie, she finished packing and looked around at her room for the last time. An impersonal space without even a picture of her girls. She had none around the house. Fear she might have to suddenly leave, making her paranoid about leaving images behind.

How would she explain to the girls that they had to leave and wouldn't be coming back? Perhaps the latter could be done while at sea where they had distraction.

The twins shared a room, painted a light pink, trimmed in white, but that was where the soft girliness ended. They'd hung a chart of the periodic table and installed a glow-in-the-dark package of stars on the ceiling, replicating the constellations. The shelves of books didn't hold fanciful tales of dragons or adventure but science and geography.

A shakeup in their routine might not be a bad idea. She'd been wondering if they were missing out on having fun of late. A cruise might be just the thing they needed.

She leaned down and shook Mae first. "Wake up."

Mae grumbled.

She shook her again. "Wake up, Mae. We have to go somewhere." When her daughter stirred, she then subjected Lin to the same nudging.

"Let's go, girls. We have to get moving."

"Why?" Mae said on a jaw-cracking yawn. "It's the middle of the night."

"It's actually just one a.m." Odd how it felt later. "You need to get up and pack."

"I wanna sleep." Lin flopped face-first onto her bed.

"You can sleep on the plane."

"We're flying?" Mae's eyes popped wide. "Where? Why?"

"It's a surprise."

The girls stared at Portia, but it was Lin who stated, "We don't like surprises."

Portia knew that. The girls preferred routine. But, sometimes, life wasn't smooth and predictable. They needed to know how to handle it when that happened. "Too bad. So sad. It's a surprise. Be ready to leave in fifteen minutes." She gave them a reasonable but short amount of time, meaning they had boundaries they could now use to structure their next move.

"That's too soon," Lin wailed, slinging her legs out of the bed.

Whereas Mae cocked her head. "For our clothing, what kind of climate are we aiming for?"

The intelligence in her girls sometimes astonished, but it always made her proud because it showed that they knew how to think. "Wear a jacket, but pack for warm weather and water."

"What about school?" Lin demanded, turning from her dresser.

"Screw school. We're going on an impromptu holiday." Portia smiled as she left their room, hoping they bought her fake gaiety. She wanted to be excited, but anxiety filled her. This wasn't a holiday.

What if Ronin knew? She couldn't believe how intensely the thought bothered her.

Her phone rang. Mother.

She answered. "Do you have our flight booked?"

"I do, plus...I've found you a husband."

"Excuse me?"

"An extra bodyguard for the trip. He'll act as your husband to confuse things a bit further."

"I don't need a stranger dogging our steps," she grumbled. "And how will I explain it to the girls? No."

"He's got a cover story. Don't worry."

"Forget it. I don't need a man mucking things up."

A knock sounded at the door, and Portia froze on the bottom step.

Marie chortled. "Oh, good. He's there."

"Who?"

"Your new husband, of course."

Joanna, a gun down by her side, was the one to answer the door.

And who should be the one standing on the step?

"Ted!"

CHAPTER SEVEN

THE SHOCK on Macey's face had Ted grimacing. He was still having a hard time reconciling the nerdy girl he once knew with the one that took him down and calmly spoke on her phone of hiring a cleanup crew and taking care of Chen.

A fucking cleanup crew to handle the men she'd killed.

Who the hell was she? What had she become?

These thoughts ran through his head as he succumbed to the drugs she'd injected him with back in that alley. Even now, he still felt the lethargy trying to control his mind and limbs.

At the time it'd happened, he'd never bothered to fight back. It would have wasted time, precious seconds where drugs spiraled throughout his system.

Rather than risk yet another needle, Ted chose to feign sleep, allowing his body to go limp. As he fell, he slipped his hand inside his gi and into the pocket where he kept a Narcan dose. He'd been keeping one close by for years now. He'd seen one too many addicts twitching on the streets and in the alleys of this neighborhood to ever go without. A long time ago, he used to be that guy drooling mindlessly after a fix. It took a friend dying during a binge in his old addict days after he'd left the military to realize that he might as well put a gun to his head because all he was doing was killing himself. Slowly. Had he survived the war in the Middle East to kill himself when safe at home?

He chose to get clean, and once he managed to get past those first few hard years, started helping others. He'd had to use the Naloxone five times since he started carrying it. Five lives saved. Not enough to rid him of his nightmares, but it helped.

And now his habit would hopefully save his life.

He made sure to land on his belly, surprised when she actually grabbed his head and made sure he didn't smash down face-first. As Macey spoke to someone, he managed to subtly inject himself, the Narcan countering the opioid making him lethargic.

How had he ever thought this sluggishness felt good. He concentrated on the pain in his body, his hand wedged between cracked asphalt and his heavy frame. His cheek against the same dirty ground.

Listened as Portia walked away and lied to someone on the phone. *I am most certainly not her boyfriend.*

Any thought he'd had of asking her out fled. She might be cute, but he drew the line at women who injected men. Not once, but twice! Had she given him a double dose of sleeping shit?

Had who what?

Ted blinked as he realized he lay on the ground.

Why am I on the ground?

She...

The elusive thought skittered away, and he pushed up from the pavement. He was in the alley behind his place. A car was parked. Engine off. A fancy Civic done up sport-style with its emerald accents.

Taotie's car.

Had he shown up at the studio? It was too early in the month. Ted staggered to his feet and glanced at the studio's rear door—closed, but was it locked? He hoped not as he glanced down at his bare feet. Why hadn't he put on shoes?

How had he come here? Ted winced and rubbed at his temples. They pounded fiercely. Staggering only a little, he approached the car, empty of occupants. He paused by the trunk.

Stared at it. For a moment, he saw a woman slamming it shut before turning to him.

Portia...

A name he didn't recognize.

His hand hovered over the metal. Did he want to see what was inside?

I need to remember.

He used the cuff of his gi to prevent him from leaving a fingerprint on the trunk release.

It popped open. He blinked at the sight and slammed the trunk shut.

Wiped it quickly with his sleeve and whirled to see if anyone else was in the alley. Not on the ground level but there were more than a few windows above.

Shit.

He hoped his feet didn't leave too much trace evidence behind as he did a stumble jog to the far end of the lane, but rather than circling around to enter his dojo from the front, he aimed for a two-story building across from it. His friend's apartment would be empty since he was on vacation. Mark had given Ted the access code to his place and asked him to water his plants. Given he couldn't remember a damned thing, he thought it prudent to use it.

The code took a few tries to enter, long enough that the sirens approaching had him sweating. Sweating was good. It would dissipate the drugs swirling inside him.

The moment he entered, he quickly headed for the kitchen for a glass of water. He chugged it and then another, knowing he had to flush his system. He then snared an energy drink from the fridge for the caffeine rush. He kept blinking. His lids were still kind of heavy. He didn't want to sleep.

He parked himself by the window overlooking the street. There was his dojo, the window lit up. What time was it?

A glance at the clock showed it past ten. He was done with classes for the night. And it was Monday... No, that didn't feel right. *It's Thursday.* He frowned. The shake of his head didn't help the fog creeping in.

He blinked, froze, a can of energy soda halfway to his mouth.

Where am I?

Why was he watching his studio?

How had he gotten into Mark's apartment?

It had been a while since he'd suffered a blackout. He took stock of himself, dressed in his gi, holding a can of pure caffeine and staring out the window.

Obviously watching. He was just in time to see a woman, someone who looked an awful lot like a chick he used to know in high school, as she crossed the street. She was clearly visible in the one streetlight before she got into a car parked on the sidewalk right below Mark's window.

Sure looks a lot like Macey.

Portia.

He frowned at the name and watched as she took off like a bat out of hell.

Because she feels guilty she drugged me.

Say what? The thought slipped through his fingers, so he drank another can of caffeine overload and put a call in to a friend. His old army buddy, Ben, answered on the second ring.

"Hey, fucker, how come you're not online yet? I thought we were playing at eleven."

Eleven. But it was only—his gaze slewed to the clock, and he saw it creeping past the eleven-thirty mark.

And wasn't this the wrong day of week? *It's...* Monday? Thursday?

This wasn't a blackout. The gritty texture in his mouth, and the slippery threads of memory only confirmed it. "Ben, I need your help. Something happened to me."

"What?" Ben's voice turned serious.

"I don't know." Ted seriously didn't remember. "It's like something is messing with my memories. Hiding them from me, like with a heavy curtain." A fog. It sometimes thinned enough for him to see, but mostly obscured, making him freak out a bit.

"Drugged?"

"Feels like it." He rubbed the back of his hand, felt a twinge and looked down to see a needle mark pinpricking the skin. "I think someone injected me with something."

"I'm not surprised. I was going to warn you about her when we played."

"Warn me about who?"

"Portia Stalone, aka Tiger Mom."

"I don't know who you're talking about."

"You don't remember sending me a message last night, asking me to look into Portia Stalone? She's a chick you used to know as Macey Munroe."

"Macey? Macey's dead."

"Not according to you."

Ted rubbed his forehead, the fog thick on his memories. "Better tell me what you know because I seem to have forgotten a few things. Last I recall, it was Monday."

"Try Thursday."

"I'm missing three days!?" he couldn't help but exclaim.

"That would be Tiger's doing."

"Tiger? What the fuck are you talking about?" Having Ben on the other line helped him to focus his thoughts but not enough to understand what was happening."

"First, let's go back to Macey Munroe. What do you remember about her?"

"Not much. And it doesn't matter. She's dead." A

shame. He'd had a crush on the smart girl in high school. Found her naturally pretty, and she'd not changed. Her hair was darker than before, but just as beautiful, and she had two very cute daughters. His eyes widened. "Macey's not dead! She came to my studio." Images flashed in his head. One in particular stuck. "Macey injected me with something." He glanced at his hand.

"Again, not surprised, given her rep. You should count yourself lucky you're still alive."

"What are you talking about?"

"You messed with Tiger Mom. Renowned for her ability to handle jobs, sometimes with just a single drop."

"She's a drug dealer?"

"No, more like an apothecary."

"What did she inject me with?"

"My guess would be something to affect your short-term memory."

"Why would she try and make me forget her?"

"Because running into you was probably a mistake. A link to her past that she'd rather not have forged."

"She's hiding from something."

"You mean someone."

Ronin. For a second, Ted heard a name but lost it. "How do you know her?"

"BBI has a file on her." BBI, as in Bad Boy Inc, agency for elite mercenaries that could solve any problem. Ted used to freelance for them, still did when the nightmares became too much and he needed an outlet. "Turns out, your high school girlfriend works for a sister agency."

"Which one?"

"The Killer Moms."

Ted snorted. "You've got to be kidding me. Macey Munroe is a mercenary?" Personally, Ted had never met any of the KM operatives, but rumor had it the agency only employed single mothers in need. They also had a reputation for only going after the worst of the worst.

And Macey was one of them?

"It's kind of a good thing you called because I was about to get ahold of you. Tiger's handler is not happy about you poking around, looking for info on Tiger."

"Who is she hiding from?"

"Ever heard of a man named Ronin?"

It sounded familiar. Ted kept watch out the window as a dark-paneled van with tinted windows rolled into the alley. "No. Who is he?"

"Ronin is a Chinese mobster with several bounties on his head. But so far, no one's managed to do the deed."

"A badass."

"The baddest."

"What's Macey to him?"

"She's his wife. Or was. The official story was that on her way to a doctor's appointment, a rival gang kidnapped her. In the attempt, everyone died. Including Macey. Or so everyone thought, including her husband, Ronin."

The realization drew a low whistle. "She chose being dead over being married or attempting a divorce?" The reason why hit him a second later. "She has two daughters. His, I assume."

"She was pregnant when the helicopter crashed."

"Does this Ronin guy know she's alive?"

"No idea. But I imagine seeing you, someone from her past, triggered her into acting."

"She tried to make me forget." For a second, he saw bodies in the trunk of a car. Then another flash of Macey slamming it shut. "She knew Taotie."

"Who?"

Ted shook his head. "A neighborhood thug." She'd killed Taotie and Eddie, but not Ted. Why?

A flash of orange in the window caught his attention. A glance had him gaping in disbelief at the flames licking at the windows of his dojo. Fuck.

There went his business, his home. Good thing he had insurance. Bad thing he currently had nowhere to live.

Because of Macey.

At this point, some would have chosen to be angry. She'd come into Ted's life and fucked it up: drugging him, killing people associated to him, and now burning everything he owned.

Yet he saw the desperation in each act. The fear.

He couldn't resist, he had to do something. "I want to help her." Despite what she'd done. Because of it. A woman who would fight that hard shouldn't do so alone.

"Let me see if her handler is interested in borrowing your services."

"I don't need money."

"If we tell them that, they'll say no for sure. They can be prickly in that sense."

"Do what you have to. I want to help."

It turned out there was no argument needed. Once

Ben reached out to Portia's handler, she was delighted to have Ted on board, and contacted him directly.

He answered the unknown number. "Hello?"

"So, you're the Ted who completely ruined poor Portia's life."

Way to pour on the guilt. "Not on purpose. Who is this?"

The smooth reply was, "Call me Mother. After all, you're about to become my son-in-law."

"Excuse me."

"A little bird told me you wanted to help."

"I do."

"Excellent. Then stop talking and listen. Once we hang up, you're to go straight to Portia's house and demand she give you the counter-remedy."

"She has one?"

"Of course. We didn't develop this forgetful serum for nothing. It's often used by our agents in the field in case they're ever captured or questioned with a truth tonic. Can't have them blabbing secrets, now can we?"

"I'll remember everything?"

"Yes. Now if you don't mind, we don't have much time. She's preparing to flee as we speak."

"She's in danger?" The thought kept him focused.

"Very, which is why having you along playing husband and father will be perfect."

"I hardly look like the twins' father," he remarked, his recollection having the girls with Asian features.

"Because you were infertile and adopted. You'll have time to work on that story during the cruise." Marie then went on to tell him the entire cover story. In a nutshell, he was going on a vacation with Macey/Portia and her kids. His job was to act as an extra layer of protection.

If Portia didn't slam the door in his face.

"What are you doing here?" she snapped upon seeing him.

"Hey, Macey. Portia. I don't know what I should call you." But seeing her triggered yet more memories. Of her cradling his head right after she'd drugged him. Remorse or wishful thinking?

"Go away. I don't have time for this."

"Can't leave. I'm here to help you."

"Oh, hell no, you're not," she muttered before turning her back and marching into another room, a phone to her ear. "Mother! Don't you dare hang up! Argh."

With Macey gone, Ted eyed the steely-eyed and haired woman at the door.

He held out his hand. "Hi, I'm Ted."

"That's what I figured," she said, eyeing him in his trendy clothes, the only thing he'd managed to find in Mark's closet. His packed bag held more of the same. "Joanna. Aunt. Former special forces. Hurt my girls, and they will never find your body."

The threat might have intimidated someone else, but it actually brought a smile. He didn't have to pretend to be meek anymore. "Also former special forces, and now a freelancer for hire."

The gaze turned appraising. "I hear BBI vouched for you."

"I work for them from time to time when I'm not teaching people martial arts basics." He still held out his hand. She eyed it for a moment and then gave it a firm squeeze.

"Good to know you're not useless."

"I guess you know why I'm here?" he stated.

"Judging by the yelling I hear going on in the other room,"—one-sided yelling as Macey ranted about the stupid plan—"Mother wants you to pretend to be her husband."

"Macey doesn't sound happy about it."

"Give her a bit to cool down. She's a bit frazzled. What happened tonight rattled her."

He tapped his temple. "I wouldn't know."

"Oh, crap, I forgot. Marie said to give this to you." Joanna pulled out a syringe. "She figured Portia might not do it if asked."

The injection was barely a prick and didn't come with instant memories.

"It might take a little bit to work," Joanna said, putting the needle away.

"But I *will* remember?"

Joanna rolled her shoulders. "Eventually."

Good, because the gaps were annoying. "When do we move out?" he asked.

"Soon. We don't think Ronin knows her whereabouts yet, so we'll depart quickly and get out of reach before that even happens."

"You're coming with us?"

"Yes. You'll refer to me as Aunt Joanna. Childless spinster, who lives with the family and helps with the girls."

"Are you my aunt or hers?"

"Hers. She knows me better."

"Better than I know my fake wife. Wouldn't it be better to pretend we're boyfriend and girlfriend?"

"Only pretend?" Joanna queried.

"What?"

"I take it you're not dating?" Before he answered, Joanna laughed. "I knew she was lying."

"Speaking of lies, what are we telling the girls? Mother didn't really cover more than their names. Lin and Mae. Something I feel like I should already know. Will they know to play along with the charade that I'm their daddy?"

"I'll handle my daughters." Macey returned, angry spots of color in her cheeks. "You need to leave."

"Nope." He shook his head. "I might not remember much yet, but I do know it's my fault your cover was blown. Which means, I owe it to you to make it right." He wasn't a man who liked to have a debt.

"Chen made it impossible for me to stay, not you."

"Chen?" he said questioningly, only to suddenly remember seeing Taotie's dead body in a trunk.

"I don't have time for this," she exclaimed.

"Don't you dare act all mad at me. You're the one who stuck me with not one but two needles," he reminded. But she'd also cradled his head on his way down to meet the pavement.

"Did I really? Because if I had done it properly, you'd still be drooling. Not to mention, you wouldn't remember me or even what you had for your last meal."

"I'm resistant to drugs." Years of doing them had built up a tolerance. He didn't mention the Narcan.

"And Mother had me give him the counter-dose," Joanna added.

"Why would you do that?" she exclaimed, flinging her hands. "He was supposed to forget."

"But I didn't, and now I'm here to help," he said, trying to soothe her agitation.

"By what, stressing me out?"

"Your mother said if we follow the plan—"

Macey slashed a hand. "I don't give a damn about the plan. We are not playing husband and wife."

"It'll help your cover if you don't look single."

"As if I need a man. I can take care of myself. Better than you." The implication was clear.

His turn to press his lips. "You think I'm useless."

"I don't just think, I saw it. How many times did you let Chen and his cronies make you grovel?"

The more he recalled what had happened, the better he understood her disdain. He grimaced. "I'm not weak. What you saw wasn't the real me."

"What I saw was a man willing to let a lowlife like Chen walk all over him." She sneered. "If you thought Chen was bad, Ronin is a thousand times worse."

"I learned in the war to pick my battles, and if I couldn't win, to make sure I lived to fight another day.

"You're a soldier?"

"Was. Honorable discharge."

Her gaze held a tad bit less disdain as she eyed him. "Rank?"

"Classified."

Joanna jumped in. "He's BBI-approved."

Definitely eyed him with more interest. Macey

crossed her arms. "This isn't a game. The stakes are deadly."

"I know."

"Doubtful." She continued to eye him. "I assume you can fire a gun."

"Yeah."

"Do you have one?"

"Not currently. My studio suffered a mishap." The barb hit home, and she bit her lower lip.

"I am sorry about that. I never meant to drag you into my problems."

"No worries. Insurance will cover the damages, and I was thinking about selling the business anyhow."

"You—" She would have said more, but the girls chose that moment to appear at the top of the stairs, Lin exclaiming, "Sir Ted, what are you doing here?" Mae, on the other hand, glanced at him then her mother and frowned. As for Joanna, she disappeared somewhere.

"Why is he here?" Mae asked. "I thought we were going on vacation."

Before Macey could make the plan more difficult, Ted jumped in. "We are. All of us together. And to make it super interesting, I am going as your dad."

Macey uttered an odd sound. He almost checked to see if she was choking.

Lin spoke for her. "Did you and Mother get married?"

"Not exactly." He didn't like lying, but the way Marie had explained it, he'd better give the twins a good reason for the act or he'd have to be prepared to tell the truth.

With just the little he knew, he could see why Macey wanted to keep the twins' past hidden. So, he wove an elaborate plot, conceived by Marie.

He rubbed his hands. "So, technically, this vacation is a present from me. I won a trip for me and my family."

"Then why aren't you taking your family?" Mae asked, hitting the bottom of the stairs and dumping a bulging knapsack on the floor.

"Because I don't have one." The honest truth. "I'd planned to go all by myself, but then I ran into your mom." He smiled at her, more mischievously than necessary as he caught her grinding her teeth. "I always did have a thing for her in high school." Still true. "And I thought, *Ted, when will you ever get the chance to not only woo the hottest and smartest girl you ever knew but also play daddy to some incredible talented young ladies?*"

Lin preened, and Mae smirked. "You want us to lie."

"Um. No. Er, that is—"

"We only need to pretend for the length of the trip," Macey declared, and he had to wonder if the girls saw through her fake smile.

"I've always wanted a daddy." Lin clasped her hands, and he heard Macey suck in a breath.

Mae proved more pragmatic. "You want us to perpetrate fraud."

His brows almost took flight. Big word for a little kid.

"It's just a white lie," Macey insisted.

It was Joanna who returned a barked, "Stop mollycoddling the little coconspirators. Can't you see they're playing you. They're old enough to get it. So, listen up, you brats. We got a chance to go on a free trip. The tickets are already paid for, so either someone uses them, or it goes to waste. Why not us? It'll be fun. We'll spend time together, take some pics and hang out. Sound good?"

"What about school?" Mae wouldn't give up.

Macey snorted. "You're taking grade ten algebra. I think you can manage a few days off."

"What of our other lessons? Will Ted still be our teacher?" Lin asked, batting her lashes as if she had dust caught in them.

"If you want to, then we can practice every day. Maybe even twice a day," he said, crossing a finger over his chest.

The girls grinned and, in tandem, said, "We can't wait, *Daddy.*" With a giggle, they ran off to the kitchen with Joanna leading the way. "Anyone need a jelly sandwich before we go?"

It left him alone with Macey, who hissed her displeasure. "I can't believe you just did that."

"You mean get your girls on board with the plan? You're welcome."

"They're my daughters. You had no right to throw that at them."

"Because I knew you wouldn't."

"This will never work. No one will ever believe we're married." Her nose wrinkled.

"On the contrary, we're already bickering like we've been together forever. Now, should I call you *honey*, or would you prefer *baby*?"

"How about neither?"'

"Couples always have nicknames for each other."

"I'm partial to *asshole.*" Said with a sweet smile.

"That might draw a little more attention than you like. I've always seen myself as more of a *pookie*."

She blinked. "You must have suffered some kind of injury when you were in the army because you are nuts."

"PTSD and other issues, but I'm doing better now." Although, if they would be in close proximity, he might have to tell her about the nightmares.

Her phone rang. She eyed the number and dragged him into an office, then slid the door closed and answered on speakerphone.

"I can't believe you hung up on me!" Macey exclaimed.

"Just figured I'd give you some time to come to your senses." Mother declared, her voice the same familiar purr of before.

"My senses are fine. He needs to leave. He's going to ruin everything."

"Your confidence warms me," Ted said, clasping his chest.

Macey tossed him a glare. "Not helping."

"Stop whining and be nice to your husband. BBI is loaning him to us at a most excellent rate."

"How the hell did Ted end up working for Bad Boy Inc?"

He knew that answer. "I was in a prison camp with one of their agents for a few weeks. You might know him. Ben?"

She pursed her lips.

"Do you know Devon and Mason and the gang?" he asked.

"I know them." She rubbed her forehead. "This world is starting to feel mighty small. Too small."

He understood that feeling. What were the chances she'd run into one let alone two people from her past in such a short time *and* in the same place?

"Would you feel better if I said, as far as I know, Ronin knows nothing yet?" Mother stated.

"Not really. Has anyone located Chunk yet?"

"Chunk?" Ted asked before he clued in. "You mean Ralph?"

Macey turned a sharp gaze on him. "What do you know about him? Where can he be found?"

"With Taotie, usually." But Taotie was dead in a trunk of a car that had been cleaned. Remembering it all meant that Ted was only *more* determined to help—and nag Macey. He preferred her angry to worried. "Given he smells like fried chicken a lot, maybe a restaurant?"

"That's not helpful," she snapped. "If you can't help, then keep that mouth of yours shut."

"Be nice, or people won't believe that you and your old flame are married," Mother interjected.

"We never dated," Macey growled.

"Nope, which is why we moved so quickly when we reconnected." Ted put a hand to his chest.

"I can't work with him," Macey declared. "He's already getting the story wrong. We are supposed to be married, not reuniting."

"The married couple with adopted children will be your primary cover story," Marie declared. "But if you do, in fact, run into someone you know from your current life, then the secondary tale, which is the one the girls are most likely to believe, is that you reconnected, and when Ted mentioned he had free tickets, you decided to be impulsive and go on a trip."

"I don't see why we can't just pretend that Daddy got sick so just the girls and me could go."

"He's going, and that's final. Or have you forgotten that if Ronin is aware of everything that's happened, then Ted is in as much trouble as you?"

Ted could have explained that he'd be fine. It wouldn't be hard for him to uproot and start over elsewhere, and yet the more Macey fought to send him away, the more determined he was to remain.

"This is only temporary," Macey growled.

"Break my heart." He clutched his chest. "And here I thought our make-believe family would live happily ever after." He deserved the dark look she tossed him.

He smiled.

"I want him gone by the end of this cruise."

"If we're lucky, by the end of the cruise, Ronin won't be a problem anymore," Mother stated.

"As if we'll have any better luck this time. You know he's too well guarded." Macey slumped in a chair that rolled slightly on the wood floor.

"If you can't get close, why not hire a sniper?" he asked.

"Gee, why didn't we think of that?" she snapped.

"Surely, he's not that well guarded."

The way Macey turned from him told him just how stupid the remark was. Obviously, he must be, or she wouldn't live in fear like this.

Knock, knock.

It was Joanna. "It's time to go. I'll drive."

Exiting the den, he noticed the girls standing solemnly by Joanna's side. Lin clutched a book, while Mae looked around before saying, "Our next house shouldn't have the staircase facing the front door. It's bad feng shui."

With those words, the girls marched off, and he could see the devastation in Macey's face.

They knew they weren't coming home.

CHAPTER EIGHT

TED GOT to ride shotgun in the front of the van with Joanna behind the wheel, while Portia took the very back row, leaving the girls in the middle, each in their own captain's seat, headphones on, watching documentaries on their tablets. Lin was into pyramids these days, while Mae chose something on hunting. Odd. She'd never shown an interest in the outdoors before.

Only pure strength of will held Portia together. A screaming panic beat within her as the day she'd dreaded finally arrived. Ronin might, at this very moment, be sending people looking for her. If Ralph had spoken, he'd have feelers out at the very least, digging for tidbits. A good thing she'd kept her presence as innocuous as possible. Lived in a neighborhood where no one spoke to each other. The hedges kept things private. No one brought pies over when they moved in. No one hosted barbecues.

The private school had her on file as being against her children's names or likenesses being used in any public way. The medical institute she worked for had hired her under a company name.

The passports in her purse were for Maevis and Linette Hogan. She had to wonder if Ted would be a Hogan too by the time they boarded the ship. Marie would probably make sure of it. Or BBI would.

It blew her mind to find out that Ted even knew Bad Boy Inc, let alone worked with them. What were the chances? Mae could probably figure it out, she was a whizz at math.

Glancing at Ted, Portia still had a hard time reconciling what she knew. The concept of the Ted who'd caved meekly to Chen, versus the knowledge of him being a soldier. He'd not shown many guts during the confrontation with Chen. A front, or so he claimed. Had she known he would fight, she might have handled things differently, yet he'd basically kowtowed until the very end. Then again, it wasn't as if she needed his help.

She'd had things perfectly well in hand until he'd shown up. And now, Mother expected her to work with him.

Husband, indeed.

Too late to change now. The plan had been set in motion, and Mother did what she did best. Coordinated.

A fellow with an envelope met them in the parking garage of the airport the moment they arrived. He handed the package over and then kept walking.

Opening it, Ted slid out a new identity: Theodore Hogan. Driver's license. Passport. Credit cards. There were even matching wedding rings, his and hers.

He held out the circlet of white gold. "May I?"

Portia's first impulse was to scream, "no," and hide her hand behind her back. Yet the girls watched with wide eyes. She mustn't let them know that anything was amiss.

Her hand trembled a bit as he slid the slim metal onto her finger. It didn't weigh her down like her last ring had. The action didn't go unnoticed.

"Who sent the rings?" Mae asked. Nothing ever got past her.

"Me. As soon as Ted invited us, I ordered them special for this trip. Just like we all have new names." No time like the present to tell the girls. She whipped out the passports and handed them to the twins. "Those are your names for the duration of our vacation."

Mae wrinkled her nose. "Maevis. Really?"

"Lucky. Isn't that the vampire girl from Transylvania. I sound like an old lady." Lin's lips turned down.

"I think Linette is very pretty," Ted declared. "Let me carry that for you." He held out his hand for both the girls' bags. Lin handed hers right over, but Mae hesitated for a second. He put one on each shoulder, then grabbed his duffle in one hand and Portia's suitcase with the other.

"I can carry it," she argued.

"I am the man of the family. I'll do it. It's my job."

"It's sexist," she remarked. "How come you're not taking Joanna's?"

"Because, as my niece, that falls on you." Joanna gestured to the much larger case. A hefty one.

"What the heck did you pack?" Portia grumbled as she dragged it along.

"Sunscreen." And probably parts to assemble a

weapon. Joanna wasn't one to go anywhere unarmed, but airports tended to frown on actual guns and knives, so cleverness was required.

Despite Portia's paranoia—*Is that guy by the magazine rack watching us? Is that security guard calling in reinforcements?*—they had no problems in the airport itself. This time of night proved rather quiet.

Too quiet.

It made her twitchy. Their flight would be leaving within an hour, taking them to an airport where they'd have only a thirty-minute window to make their connection, and only after they falsely checked in for another flight.

That she'd have to lie didn't bother, it was the fact that she had the girls with her that caused a flutter. They would ask questions. They would see something was amiss.

With her nerves stretched tautly, she parked the girls with Joanna at their gate and paced the terminal.

To her annoyance, Ted stalked with her.

"Why are you following me?"

"We should take this time to iron out the details of our story."

"I'd rather avoid talking to people at all."

"That might work," he said in a musing tone. "Tell people to fuck off because we're so in love."

She almost stumbled. "No one will believe it."

"They will if we're constantly caught necking in the halls."

"There will be no necking."

"Hand-holding?" he said with a hopeful lilt. His attitude made no sense.

"Why are you so calm about this?"

"One of us should be. You're a mess," was his bald statement.

She halted and glared. "Can you blame me?"

"You're no good to anyone if you're going to be agitated."

"I think I have earned that right."

"Save it for later when we're not being observed."

"Someone is watching us?" Her gaze slewed left and right.

"Could you be more obvious?"

The rebuke stung, but she wasn't about to apologize. "People are always looking around suspiciously in airports."

"I meant watching on cameras. Security monitors all the public areas."

"I know."

"Then act like it. We're supposed to be a married couple going on vacation with our children."

"What would you suggest I do? Sit and read them a story while you browse a newspaper?" she retorted sarcastically.

"You can be agitated but have a reason. We'll hit that little pharmacy by gate nine and grab something for upset stomachs."

"I'm not taking any drugs."

"Pretend. Do you know how to make believe?" His sarcasm hung thick.

"Don't talk to me like I'm a moron."

"Then snap out of it and show me why KM thinks you're worth hiding."

"Am I not playing the part of wife well enough? Oops. Bad me." She stepped closer, enough that she had to tilt her head to keep her gaze on him. A wary look entered his eye.

"What are you doing?"

"We've been fighting. So now I'm being a good wife and making up." She nipped his chin, her lips scraping on the stubble.

He trembled. "Making up by biting me?"

"Is this better?" She lifted her lips and brushed her mouth against his, meaning for it to be a light embrace. He had other plans. His arm slid around her waist and snared her, pulling her close. His mouth slanted over hers, took a feathery touch and ignited it.

The kiss left her breathless, her lips tingling, other parts of her heating...

"That's better, wife," he purred against her mouth. "You're forgiven. Go fetch me that Alka-Seltzer while I grab a newspaper." He twirled her from him and gave her a slap on the ass as he pushed her in the direction of the pharmacy. But he remained close, browsing a magazine display as she bought a few things. Did anyone else notice how he managed to watch in all directions, paying special attention to their gate?

She paid for the stuff and sauntered back his way. "See anything, oh mighty spy?"

"Not yet."

"Rather than hovering over me, you should be guarding the girls."

"You're the one in more imminent danger."

"Except I care less about me than them," she snapped as he kept pace by her side.

He had his hands shoved into his pockets. "And I'm sure they feel the same about you. How about we do our best to keep you all safe?"

She sighed. "I'm sorry. I don't mean to be a bitch. I just wish we didn't have to live like this."

"Your mother didn't seem to think Ronin knew yet."

"I can't take the chance."

"Let's assume then that he knows. He'll obviously have pictures of you he can use to track you down."

"They won't work." She put a hand to her nose. "We had it shaved to change the shape." She touched her chin. "More squared. With the hair, it makes any old images of me invalid when it comes to facial recognition software."

"I recognized you. Taotie, too."

"People have an ability to see beyond measurements in person. Computer programs don't." She shrugged. "Or so we're hoping."

"But if Ralph talks..."

"Then Ronin will know I'm alive, and he won't stop looking until he finds us. We kind of stand out." She glanced down to their gate, where Joanna sat with the girls. A white woman with Asian-featured children always drew attention.

"Going back to my argument, let's say he locates you, is he likely to hurt his daughters?"

She chewed her lower lip. "No. He's usually very big on family."

"Meaning he won't attempt to harm them. But you..."

He slewed a glance her way. "He'll be pissed at you. A man like that will want revenge."

And she doubted that revenge would be quick. "The good news is, I doubt he'll kill me. I betrayed him. He'll want to savor my terror." She said it matter-of-fact, mostly because over the years, she'd grown used to the familiar fear. How many times had she been convinced that he was coming for her? How many nights had she woken gripped in a terror so deep, she'd sat in the twins' bedroom, gun in her lap, back to the wall, convinced that he was coming to get them?

Why wouldn't he just die and spare her the grief?

"Aw, sweetheart." Ted's tone, it sounded...sad? She eyed him. He shook his head. "And you wonder why I want to help. I am not about to let a sadistic prick hurt you."

"What you want doesn't matter. But it might get you killed. If he finds out I'm alive, he won't stop searching until he finds me." Left unsaid? *And makes me pay*.

"Only if he finds out. There's a chance he won't. Maybe Ralph will keep his mouth shut, or your agency will find him before he can blab."

"Ronin knows." She could feel it in her gut.

9

RONIN

THE PHONE CALL had been recorded and almost discarded. Except for one thing.

A name that caught the attention of his right-hand man, mostly because it was one forbidden to be spoken.

Macey.

And yet, of late, it kept appearing. First, in the recent database queries on his late wife. Then in that voicemail claiming she wasn't dead.

Could it be true?

Even though it was probably some kind of shake-down, Ronin had to know for sure. One of his people contacted the street thug from America, a fellow named Ralph. Of course, when asked to confirm his statement, he had no pictures. No other witnesses because Ralph claimed Macey had killed Chen and someone named Eddie, too.

His Macey, a murderer? The very idea seemed laugh-able. He clearly recalled her expression the night he'd knifed his cousin. Repulsed. Afraid. Horrified. Not once had she ever raised a hand, and only barely ever used her voice. The perfectly demure and obedient wife, pregnant with his daughters, horrifically taken from him by his enemies.

Or so he'd thought. What if she'd not died in a botched kidnapping attempt? Could she have been hiding from him this entire time?

Defying him and keeping his children from their father?

Despite the inanity, the idea fermented, rousing an elation in him that he might get her back—and show her the error of her ways. But at the same time, he didn't believe it. Because then he'd have to accept the ridiculous idea that she'd managed to kill Chen. Highly unlikely. The night she'd disappeared, it was another who'd wielded the gun that shot Chen.

Still... It wouldn't hurt to look into the situation. Ralph claimed he'd seen them at some exercise studio, and he'd not changed his story even after being questioned. Few people could resist telling the truth when the right incentive was applied via a burning brand.

A press of a button brought up a screen and his computer wizard—Kira—appeared, her hair currently a striped pink and purple, yet another piercing in her brow, her lips a flaming red.

"Boss." She snapped a piece of gum. Disrespectful, and yet so talented. But she'd soon have to be reined in without ruining her use. He couldn't have her being so casual with him.

"Find out everything you can about a Flamingo

Martial Arts business. USA-based. Owned by a Ted Grady."

"Did you just say Ted Grady?"

"Yes. Why?"

"Because remember how you wondered who'd been looking up your wife? You'll never guess whose name appeared once I finally traced the seeker."

The coincidences kept stacking. "Why is he looking?"

"Apparently, they went to high school together."

"So, he knew her." This Ted person must have seen her, or someone he thought might be Macey, then searched for her. His inquiries on the internet were public, only barely hidden by firewalls. But more interesting was that after the regular kind of queries were exhausted, a ping arrived on the Darknet, seeking the same information. "I want to know everything about this Grady."

Next, he called in his right-hand man. "Get my jet ready."

"Where to, boss?" Jiao asked.

"San Francisco for starters. But then we'll be heading to the east coast."

"On it."

"Wait," Ronin said as Jiao went to leave. "Also, locate Chen. I want him brought in for some questioning." Ralph had claimed that Chen was dead, but Ronin wasn't quite ready to simply take him at his word.

"Aye, aye, boss." Jiao saluted and left. A solid man for the task, but not his former best friend. A friend who'd failed him.

Ronin leaned back in his chair. He steepled his fingers, staring at the window and yet not seeing the stunning vista. He could think of nothing but the possibility that Macey lived.

My wife.

But, more importantly, he wondered about his children...

CHAPTER TEN

THE KICK to the ribs woke him. Ted rolled over to see a robed man standing over him, face veiled so only his eyes showed, cradling a gun in his arms.

He struggled to his feet, tired, hurt, hungry, and dehydrated. Prisoners were given the bare minimum to survive. He began to shuffle, knowing the routine. They'd take him to a tent or a cave, and someone would ask him questions in heavily accented English.

He'd offer a bullshit reply. They'd hurt him. But they wouldn't kill him. Not yet. Not if they wanted to use him as a bargaining chip.

They shuffled into the cave, his hands tied behind him, meaning he couldn't stop himself from falling face-first when his guard kicked at his knee. He toppled, smashing his chin, feeling it jolt through his skull. He tasted blood in his mouth and rolled over to look at the chair.

His seat as he'd come to think of it.

Only it had someone sitting in it.

Macey, her head held high, her expression defiant.

"Submit."

"Never." She didn't hesitate.

Ted uttered a sound that was half-moan, half-roar as she rocked from the fist that hit her.

He struggled to get to his knees. Helpless. Yet, he couldn't simply lie there.

"Down, dog." The blow to his head blurred his vision, but not enough that he didn't see the leer, the fear on her face, the—

"Ted! Ted!" The hushed whisper snapped him out of the dream—the nightmare. The sour taste of it filled his mouth, and he clenched the flesh of his thighs lest he lash out, still caught in its net.

"Ted? You were thrashing in your sleep."

"Sorry," was his low reply as he shifted in his seat. "Nightmares."

"Do you get them often."

He shrugged and looked out the window rather than at her. "Sometimes."

"I get the bad ones, too," she admitted softly. "The psychiatrist I saw said it was normal. My mind trying to deal with my anxiety."

"Because we're not anxious enough," was his snorted reply. "I usually take something to help me sleep so I don't dream."

"I can't. I don't dare slumber that deeply."

An admission that caused his chest to tighten. "Whereas I sometimes don't care if I wake up."

She sucked in a breath. "You're suicidal?"

He winced. "Not exactly. Not anymore," he quickly

explained. "After I came home from the war, I was lost for a while. Dealing with things I'd done. Things done to me." He wasn't about to spill his guts and whine about how he'd been a prisoner, tortured for weeks. How he'd killed to escape. How he'd made his torturer scream for hours before he ended his life. "I turned to drugs and alcohol. Copious amounts of it. Almost died a few times." Was always surprised when he woke up.

"Something changed," she stated.

"Yeah. I decided to stop being a whiny fucker." He winced. "That came out wrong. But it's right at the same time. I woke up one morning beside a friend—also a former soldier. Dead. In him, I saw my future. I saw..." Nothing. And he felt shame. How many had died who'd wanted to come home? How many families mourned their passing? Here he was, perfectly healthy and yet killing himself slowly. Making a mockery of their sacrifice. He cleared his throat. "I went into rehab that same day. Been clean seven years now."

"But you still have nightmares."

"I do."

To his surprise, she grabbed his hand and squeezed it. "I'm glad you found your way."

"So am I," he whispered. *So am I.*

They arrived in Texas early in the morning more than twenty-four hours after they'd left, having switched airports a few times and renting a Suburban for the last five-hour drive on their trip.

The cruise didn't leave until the next day, meaning they needed a place to crash when they arrived in the slowly waking city. Luckily, BBI had a few rental properties and allowed them the use of a villa with several bedrooms and a pool that the twins eschewed. Instead, they chose to lounge in the house, headsets on, faces glued to their tablets. Kind of like their mother, who spent a lot of time on her phone and even more avoiding him. It was as if that intimate moment on the plane had never happened.

Yet, he knew something had changed between them. It had started with the kiss. He had caught her eyeing him a few times, once even touching her lips. Had the embrace ignited her as much as it had enflamed him? He'd not expected the heated spark. Nor the urge for more.

In high school, he'd been attracted to Macey, but then again, any girl who smiled pretty much drew him. Macey, though, she had been more than just a pretty face. She'd not made any attempt to conform. She didn't wear makeup or worry about her clothes. She wore comfortable leggings, slim-fitting cowled sweaters in winter, T-shirts and jeans in spring and summer.

Even now, she remained natural, fresh-faced, her hair kept simple, usually brushed and pulled into a tail. Her clothes unassuming and not meant to draw attention to her curves. She remained smart. A woman of many talents—who still wasn't interested in him.

He shouldn't care. It was for the best. He came with his own baggage. Yet, his ego felt bruised.

Stressed, he exercised, in this case, he went for a swim. On his tenth lap—stroke, stroke, stroke, breathe— he saw little legs dangling in the water. He slowed and bobbed, recognizing Mae sitting on the edge.

"Coming for a swim?" he asked despite noting that she wore a summer dress.

She shook her head.

"Do you know how?"

A disdainful snort was his reply.

"The water is nice."

"I'm not in the mood."

A somber child, she appeared more serious than usual. "What's wrong?"

For a moment, he thought she wouldn't say. When she spoke, her words took him by surprise.

"Our house burned down."

"Oh, shit." He heaved himself out of the water and sat down beside the girl, dunking his feet beside her. "What happened? How do you know?" He didn't mention the fact that he was surprised Macey had told them.

"I saw it online."

Shit, the child had found out by accident. "That sucks."

Her head ducked. "Yeah. It happened after lunch today."

Later than he would have expected given how the cleanup crew had set fire to his dojo immediately.

"I'm sorry," he said while he scrambled for a proper reply. He obviously couldn't tell the child that the house had been burned to keep her safe.

"Why are you sorry? You didn't burn it."

"No. However, I know how horrible it is to lose everything you have." It'd happened to him a few times. Seven years clean was all well and good. The years before that, he'd made a mess of things, numerous times.

Mae cocked her head. "I guess you do know. The article said they think it might be a serial arsonist given your studio burned, too. And our school."

"Your school?" It surprised him that the cleanup crew had gone that far.

"Only the junior high wing."

"I'm sure they have a plan in place for their students while they conduct repairs."

"Maybe. Doesn't matter since we're not going back."

"What makes you say that?" he asked, cautious to not reveal anything.

"Mother packed her memory box. She usually leaves it locked up and hidden under the floor in her office."

What could he say? He knew Macey wouldn't appreciate him butting in with her daughter. Hard to believe Mae was supposed to be only ten years old. She had a maturity and an astuteness to her that meant he couldn't lie.

"I can't speak to your mother's plans, but I can assure you that she only wants what is best for you."

"Are we in danger?" Again, a direct question that saw through the subterfuge.

"What makes you think that?" he hedged.

"Three fires are more than a coincidence."

"Not really. Studies have shown that arsonists have a tendency to escalate."

"And just happen to hit three places that have one thing in common? My family?" The girl proved much too bright as she connected those dots. "We're running from something."

Would he lose his man card if he bellowed for Macey? He wanted to respect her wishes. Didn't want to meddle, but her daughter seemed determined.

"It's not my place to tell."

Which in and of itself was an admission.

Mae smiled. "You don't have kids."

"No."

"Why?" She kicked her feet in the water, light enough to agitate the surface.

The question out of the blue startled. "Because I never got married."

"Do you have a girlfriend?"

"I've had a few girlfriends, but none that stuck around."

"Why?"

He shrugged. "Guess I'm not an easy guy to be with." It didn't help that the nightmares woke them and frightened.

"Neither is Mom. She never dates."

"It's probably on account she's so busy with you and your sister, plus her work."

Mae shook her head. "It's because of our father."

"Oh. What makes you say that?" he asked, aiming for casual. What had Macey told the children about their dad?

"I know it's because of him because she never talks about him. Has no pictures, not even a wedding one. She says they got lost, misplaced by some movers. And if we ask about him, she shuts us right down." Mae slashed her hand.

"It's likely a difficult subject for her." He cast a glance over his shoulder, looking for rescue. This wasn't a conversation he should be having.

"We have a right to know about our dad," Mae declared.

"She only wants what's best for you." It sounded lame, like a cop-out. Yet no way would he tell this child that her father actually lived and might be a danger to her mother.

"Sure, she does," she replied sullenly. "You're just taking her side because you're a grown-up, too."

"Your mom doesn't seem like the type to do anything that would hurt you."

"Never said she was hurting us. There's this girl in our class, said her mom hated her dad so much, she moved away and blocked him from calling."

"I hardly think the situation is the same. Your father is no longer with us."

"Or so Mom says." Mae's next foot kick held a hint of petulance. "Do you know we've never met anyone in his family?"

"That's not uncommon. I don't have any."

"We do. On Mom's side of the family, we have a bunch of aunts. Cousins. And a grandma, too."

"Sounds like you have plenty of family members."

"Grandma adopted a bunch of them. They're not our *real* family," Mae insisted.

"Family isn't always about blood, it's about trust." His

reply was careful. He'd had his own issues for a while and had burned more than a few bridges. Saying "*sorry*" didn't always fix them, which was why even though he'd cleaned up his act and apologized, he tended to remain a loner.

"Doesn't matter if she trusts his family or not. I should be allowed to make that decision. Not her." The child sulked.

"I really think you should talk to your mom about this."

"Why? So she can lie? She's keeping a secret from us. And so are you," Mae accused.

"You and your conspiracy theories," Lin snorted a moment before she shoved her twin into the water.

Splash. As Mae screeched and flailed, Lin took her spot on the pool's edge beside Ted.

"Ignore my sister. She has issues."

"You are so dead." Mae treaded water and glared.

Lin stuck out her tongue. "Go ahead and try."

"Girls." He sounded as helpless as he felt. "Don't fight."

"You're not our daddy. You can't tell us what to do," Mae hotly declared.

"Our father is dead," Lin's rebutted.

"No, he's not."

Uh-oh. He'd have to warn Macey that Mae was on to her.

"He is so dead, and I wish you'd stop pretending he isn't," Lin huffed hotly. "I don't see what the big deal is, anyhow. All dads do is fart and tell dumb jokes."

Ted blinked. "Um, I'm pretty sure they do more than that." Then again, what would he know? He'd been raised by a single mother, his father having left to be with another woman when he was young. He hadn't seen Ted much before he died of a heart attack at forty-one.

"Dads punish bratty sisters who are mean and push their favorite daughters into the water," Mae declared.

"You looked hot. I was doing you a favor," Lin stated with a shrug of her shoulders.

"You look hot, too. You should join me."

"No, thanks. I'm not in the mood to change."

Ted knew he shouldn't do it, but seeing Mae in the pool with her sister acting smug...

He shoved Lin in, and as she bobbed to the surface ready to exclaim, he slid in and torpedoed off the bottom. When he rose, it was to hear Lin complaining, Mae laughing, and to spot Macey standing on the side of the pool, her hands on her hips.

"What's going on?"

Oh, shit.

Lin stopped her complaining, and he waited to get ratted out. Macey would kill him for daring to dunk her kid.

Instead of sentencing him to doom, the child smiled. "Mother. You should join us. The water is lovely."

"And very wet," Mae declared, splashing a hand.

"I don't have a swimsuit."

"Neither did we," Lin replied, batting her lashes.

"Maybe later." Macey turned her attention to Ted. "Can I talk to you for a minute?"

"Sure." As he stroked for the side, he heard Mae mutter, "Uh-oh. Someone is in trouble."

He heaved himself out of the water and couldn't help

but suck in his nonexistent gut as Portia's gaze licked over his slick torso. He kept in shape, but he was also conscious of his scars. It surprised him that the girls hadn't asked about them.

He grabbed a towel and scrubbed it over the damp parts. Macey looked past him as she spoke. "Something happened."

"Your house burned down. I heard."

"How did you hear?" Her gaze narrowed as she eyed her girls in the pool. "They know?"

"Don't suppose you've noticed they are super smart. And Mae's asking questions."

"About?"

"Why we really left, for starters." He left out the part where Mae didn't believe that her father was dead. Macey had enough to deal with at the moment.

"What did you tell her?"

"Nothing, so you can calm down. But she is suspicious. You're going to have to tell her something, though, because she knows this isn't a real vacation."

"We need a better story. Something they'll believe."

"What if you told them the truth?"

"The truth?" She walked away from the pool but didn't enter the house until they passed Joanna coming out. "How do I explain that? Your father isn't dead. But hey, congrats! He's a murderous, controlling crime lord that can never get his hands on you."

"Why not tell them? They're too smart. They will eventually figure it out on their own."

"Not yet."

"Then when? Mae knows you're hiding something."

Her lips compressed. "I'll handle it. You giving me advice about my kids isn't the reason I came looking for you. As you heard, my house burned down."

"Yeah, Mae mentioned it. Along with their school. Guess it's a good idea. It will eradicate DNA and fingerprint traces."

"Except for the fact that Mother didn't order it. She'd already sent in a cleaning crew to scrub those places down. Fire brings too much attention."

"They burned my studio."

"One fire is fine, three…"

"Is a warning. Shit." Ted flopped onto the couch and took a moment to absorb the information and weigh the ramifications. "If your handler didn't order it, then who set them?"

"Probably the same person who broke into my office at work and torched it."

Four fires. Only one of them sanctioned. His blood ran cold. "You think it's Ronin."

"Who else?" She paced. "It's good we left. But I am worried he'll be able to follow our trail."

"No one knows about the new identities."

She ducked her head. "Ronin will find us, it's only a matter of time."

"Seems kind of pessimistic."

"Realistic. Marie and the KM gang are good, but now that Ronin knows I'm alive, and that his girls are too, he'll stop at nothing to find us."

Her expression tugged at him, and he found himself kneeling in front of her, clasping her cold hands in his. "Don't give up."

"I haven't." It was softly said while tears glistened. She did her best to fight it, but he could see the stress taking its toll.

"Don't cry, sweetheart. You're not alone." He reached out to cup her cheek. She leaned her face into his palm, eyes closed.

His thumb stroked over her bottom lip. He drew closer.

Suddenly, there was banging as someone flung open the door and entered. "Why couldn't I be an only child?" grumbled Mae as she stalked past.

It broke the spell. Macey pulled away from him and, without a word, followed her daughter. Ted was left staring, realizing with a chill that he was doing the one thing he'd sworn not to do because it led to trouble.

Caring.

Fuck.

CHAPTER ELEVEN

AFTER THAT MOMENT OF WEAKNESS, Portia hid. She'd let her guard down with Ted.

Why? It wasn't like she needed him. And yet, while she'd held it together when she told Joanna what had happened, she'd almost fallen apart with Ted.

And he'd provided support.

Would have kissed her too if not interrupted.

She yanked her fingers from her lips as she realized she touched them again.

This really wasn't the time to be distracted. Never mind this never happened. She'd sworn off men after Ronin. Had no interest. At all.

Ted appeared to be changing that, and she couldn't say why. What she did know was that the girls seemed quite taken with him. Lin kept batting her lashes and playing cute, but Mae, Portia's smart and acerbic child, appeared to be placing trust in him. Confiding things that made Portia realize that Ted might be right. She'd soon need to tell her children the truth.

Ask forgiveness for her lies.

But...she couldn't do it yet.

Ted drove them to the port, and they lined up with the rest of the passengers to board the ship—just another family, lost in the crowd. They caused a bit of a slow-down as Joanna's presence caused a kerfuffle until her special accommodations were located. Apparently, the family suites were meant to be for two adults and up to four children. Not an aunt.

The family suite consisted of two rooms. A master bedroom of sorts, with a couch and a television, and a smaller room with its own bathroom and two double beds.

Once Portia spotted the bed situation, she declared, "The twins and I will take the smaller room."

To which Joanna snorted. "Like hell you are," she replied. "The girls and I will bunk together, while the married couple gets the suite with the king-sized mattress."

Share a room and a blanket with Ted?

"No."

"Why ever not?" Joanna said, too sweetly.

"It wouldn't be right."

"Weren't you the one telling me you were dating?"

That got some gasps. "You're dating our teacher? Since when?" Mae demanded while Lin gazed at her with accusation.

"It's not true. I, um..."

Joanna arched a brow. "You what?"

She came clean. "I lied, okay? And you know why." She glared at Joanna, who smirked.

"If we want the cover to work, then the sleeping arrangements should appear authentic."

"To who?" Portia snapped.

"Anyone who might come knocking. Crew, other passengers... We wouldn't want them to know we're not a family and take away the prize," Ted said with a slight raise of a brow and a tilt of the head in the twins' direction.

He perpetrated the lie, and Portia saw Mae rolling her eyes. She didn't buy the contest thing one bit. But he was right. If they wanted to blend in, they had to appear normal.

"Fine. You and I will share. Girls, unpack quickly so we can watch the ship leave port."

"Okay," Lin said before slamming the door shut between the rooms. Portia almost opened it up again, conscious that they were alone—with a bed. Frustrated, she whirled on Ted.

"This is a stupid idea."

"Why?"

"Because I don't want to share a room with you."

"I promise to knock before entering the bathroom, and not to leave the toilet seat up."

"There's only one bed."

"A big one. And I don't snore. Do you?"

"No."

"Then I don't see the problem. I thought you were a KM operative."

"I am."

"Aren't you supposed to be good at undercover operations?"

The rebuke stung. Why was she being such a bitch about this?

Anxiety was partially to blame, but if she dug a little deeper, she had another reason. Ted.

She'd be alone with the man. In a bedroom. Hell, sharing a bed.

She'd not done that since Ronin. Admitting it wasn't an option, but she did need to give him some kind of apology. "I'm sorry. I don't mean to snap. I'm stressed." She sat on one of the two chairs bolted to the floor.

He kneeled across from her. "You're safe for the moment. I highly doubt he knows where we've gone. Or what names we're using now."

"It's not just that. My girls. The lies." She waved a hand. "It's like a house of cards, and I'm worried it's going to come crashing down."

"Then handle it before it tumbles."

"Where do I start?" she replied bitterly.

"Mae says you won't talk about their father."

"No kidding, I don't." She uttered a short bark of laughter. "What would I say? More lies, claiming he's some kind of saint? I won't do it. Can't do it."

"Mae won't accept that forever. She wants to know about her roots."

"Then I'll fabricate something for her."

"What if she sees through it?"

Portia hung her head rather than reply.

"They're observant," he added softly.

"No shit." A sigh escaped her, leaving her limp. "I know I have to tell them something. I'm working on it."

"Better work on it faster. Mae knows you're not going

home after the cruise. I assume Lin suspects it, too. What are you going to tell them?"

"I don't know." She slumped. "How do I explain to them that everything they've known is gone because the father who's not supposed to exist will kill me and take them if he ever finds us?"

"The only real solution is for Ronin to die."

Her lips turned down. "Easier said than done."

Honk.

The ship blew its horn, announcing their departure.

"Come on, sweetheart. Let's take the girls to the top deck to watch." He held out his hand.

She eyed it and then looked him over. "What a grand idea, pookie."

He grinned. "Is that because I'm cuddly?"

"More like empty-headed like a stuffed bear." She smiled before she flung open the door. The girls lay on the bed right across from it and looked up as she entered.

"Ready to start our vacation?" she asked.

Mae pointed to her tablet. "The Wi-Fi isn't working."

"Mine either."

"Because we are on a cruise, girls." And realizing her children were snooping meant that she had activated a killswitch to shut off the Wi-Fi. She should have thought of it sooner, but she'd been so busy checking for tails. She'd not thought of the devices in their possession that could be tracked.

She'd have to get Tanya to wipe their online presence and create new ones that they could take over. Also, a sub-routine on their devices to circumvent any searches into their old lives.

But that was for later. Ted was right. The more normal they appeared, the less likely people would be to remark on them.

They spent the first day at sea, exploring the ship. Bowling. Swimming. Then a family movie that night where she and Ted shared a bucket of popcorn— unhealthy as was the box of Whoppers. Yet there was something pleasant about sitting next to him with the girls split up on either side, Joanna having chosen to explore further.

Later, Ted even helped tuck the girls into bed, carrying Lin when she began to doze at the end of the movie.

Then it was just the two of them, in a room with one bed. He grabbed a pillow and the spare blanket from the closet and tossed them onto the floor.

"What are you doing?"

"Getting comfortable," he stated as he stripped off his shirt.

Her gaze went to his flesh and the puckered scars. "How did you get those?"

Only briefly did his gaze drop to his torso. His big shoulders rolled. "War."

"One of those looks recent."

"Mission where I should have been paying more attention."

"Have you killed many people?"

He paused in the process of stripping his shorts. He wore solid-colored boxers. "A few. You?"

"More than I ever imagined. The first time, I told

myself, '*never again.*' But Mother always knows which ones I will say no to."

"You have a code?"

"Of a sort. I don't harm children or those who appear innocent."

"Whereas I used to just kill in whatever direction I was pointed." He grimaced.

"You obeyed orders."

"Yup, with no regard for whether it was right or wrong."

"Do your actions give you nightmares?"

"Sometimes." His lips turned down. "I've done a lot of bad things in my life."

"Things you regret?"

He shrugged. "Yeah, but I can't change the choices I've made. I just live in the here and now, trying to do better."

He lay on the floor in the nest he'd made. He actually planned to sleep there. Had her trepidation over them sharing been that obvious? How dare he be a gentleman!?

Portia eyed the very large bed.

"Do you sprawl?"

He lay on his back, eyes closed, hands on his chest. "No."

"Steal blankets?"

He cocked open an eye. "Not usually. Why?"

"Get in bed."

"I'm fine."

"It's a hard floor, and the bed is huge. Besides, what if someone sees?"

"The only people who will notice are your girls. What will they say if they see us sharing a bed?"

"Probably not much. Joanna, though..." She grimaced.

"Has she been hinting at you, too?" he asked.

Portia's eyes widened. "What has she said?"

"Not much, other than you need a man."

"I do not," she huffed.

"She also said you were destroying the planet with your battery usage."

As she squeaked, "She did not!" he smiled so widely, a dimple puckered his cheek.

"She might have strongly hinted that you were single, looking, and that I'd be an idiot not to notice how attractive you are."

"Joanna is going to die," she groaned.

"Die for telling the truth? You are hot. And I'm not an idiot.," he said as he rose to his feet, all six feet plus of half-naked man.

"You know what, maybe this isn't a good idea."

"Okay." He immediately dropped to the floor, meaning she uttered a sound again. "Oh, for God's sake. Get in this bed. But stick to your side. No funny business."

"I can't promise I won't have nightmares."

"Neither can I. So I guess that makes us even."

She was very aware of the mattress dipping as he lay down beside her. Far enough away that nothing touched, and yet she remained conscious of his presence. Could have reached out to touch him if she wanted. He lay on his back, completely still, and stayed that way even as his breathing evened into sleep. Eventually, she slumbered, too.

Turned out he wasn't the problem in bed. She was. Portia woke up, draped over him, the blanket tugged from his chest and wrapped around her. His skin was cold on the exposed side, whereas she was warm, snuggled against him, his arm cradling her so that his hand splayed over her hip.

An interesting position to wake up in. An embarrassing one given the twins who stood staring by the side of the bed.

CHAPTER TWELVE

TED SLEPT LIGHTLY. Had ever since his time overseas. So the moment Macey shifted in her sleep, he was awake and very much aware. As for when she snuggled against him? Pleasure and pain all at once. But a good kind of agony. He lay still as a corpse, almost afraid to breathe, because then she might move, and he didn't want that.

Eventually, her warmth seeped into him enough that he actually relaxed and managed to catch a few more hours. In a row. Without waking startled and in a sweat. Yet another reason he'd thought sleeping on the floor would be better. When he wasn't having nightmares, he suffered night terrors. Not the kind that ended in screams or thrashing. But the kind where he died in the dream and woke, momentarily paralyzed in the dark, wondering if he'd finally breathed his last.

Not this morning. Instead, for the first time in a long while, he woke to sunshine streaming through a window, and a warm body draped trustingly across his chest.

There was no noise other than what he'd expect from a ship in motion. Yet he had a strange sense of being watched. When he opened his eyes, he strangled a scream as he noticed the twins staring silently at him. How had they managed to sneak up on him? How long had they been standing there?

What did they want? He felt very conscious of the fact that he'd not worn a shirt to bed, and that their mother was intimately draped. Never mind the fact that nothing untoward had happened, the visual impression indicated otherwise. A grown man shouldn't be embarrassed, and yet, as they remained silent and staring, he couldn't help but feel judged. How should he address the situation?

He started with the basics. "Morning, girls."

"Morning, Father." The words were spoken in tandem, giving him a chill.

Macey snorted and stirred against his chest before she chided her daughters. "Girls, don't be creepy."

"Just practicing the charade, Mother," Mae declared, pretending innocence.

"We were wondering when you were getting up. It's eight o'clock, and we're hungry," Lin complained.

"Where's Aunt Joanna?"

"She went for a morning jog around six and then wanted to have a swim before people invaded the pool," Mae informed.

Joanna went on patrol while Ted lazed away in bed. He just couldn't seem to make a good impression.

"Let me shower first," Macey began to say, to immense groans.

"I can't wait that long. I'll die of hunger," Lin exclaimed, clutching her belly.

"Breakfast is the most important meal of the day, Mother." Mae lifted her chin.

Ted came to the rescue. "You shower. I'll take the girls."

Macey opened her mouth, and he was convinced that she'd say no. As were the girls, who readied their expressions to protest.

She surprised them all. "Sure. I'll meet you in the dining hall."

What?

Macey rolled out of bed, her shorts and T-shirt covering her, and yet the sexiest thing he'd ever seen. He averted his gaze and encountered that of the observant twins.

"So, *Daddy,*" Mae enunciated. "What's the plan today?"

"We'll decide over breakfast. And for that, I need pants or shorts," he declared. "Shoo, while I find my clothes." It didn't take him long to dress, but he did run into a problem of where to hide a gun. He couldn't. Not in this tropical weather that didn't allow for layers.

But they should be safe on the ship.

The breakfast was served buffet-style. While he loaded up on pancakes, bacon, hash browns and coffee, the girls chose fruit and yogurt with nuts.

He eyed their healthy plate versus his. He had to ask. "Do you ever eat junk food?" Because it occurred to him that during their trip thus far, he'd yet to see them munching on chips or candy.

"We did last night. Popcorn and licorice. But we rarely partake in processed garbage," Lin said, and he couldn't tell if it she offered her own opinion or a parroted one.

"That stuff might be processed crap, but bacon is the food of the gods," he declared, holding up a strip.

"Salty fat," Lin declared.

"Delicious," he countered.

"Yes, it is." Macey arrived sooner than expected and plucked the piece out of his hand.

"Hey! That's mine."

"Everyone knows bacon is more delicious when it belongs to someone else." She flopped into the seat beside him. "You going to finish that?"

She tugged his plate over, and the girls giggled.

"Mom. What are you doing?" Lin exclaimed.

"Since your dad forgot to get me a plate, I'm sharing his."

"Poor Daddy is going to die of starvation." Lin snickered.

"Let's get them more," Mae declared.

"Bring bacon," Ted demanded.

"And hash browns. This is good." Macey began to seriously eat his food, and he had to wonder...

"I'm surprised you're not going for the fruit like your girls."

"Usually, I would. But this is going to be a high carb kind of day."

"What makes you say that?" he asked.

"When we dock at noon at the first island on our stop,

we'll be scouting some possible new homes. Marie sent me a list while I was in the shower."

"You're going to move to the Caribbean?"

"Possibly. Depends on how we like it."

"And if you do, does that mean the cruise might be over by dinner?"

"No. It would cause too much attention for us to miss the ship's departure. But the shore leave gives us a chance to house hunt without drawing notice."

"What about your work in the States?"

"I'll find another lab, or KM will start one. I've got enough money socked away to not really worry about that stuff for a while. Have you thought about where you'll go after the cruise? You do realize you can't return to your old life, right?"

"Yeah, I know." But he'd not given it much thought.

"Are you going to be okay? Do you need help getting set up somewhere?"

He arched a brow. "Are you offering?"

"Not me, but I'm sure Mother could manage something."

"If I need anything, my buddy Ben will take care of me. But thanks."

Macey didn't reply. She stared at the buffet and the girls.

An older man with his hair combed back from a receding forehead, and a camera around his neck talked to the twins. He pointed to the device then at the girls, and Ted could see Macey readying to go mama bear on his ass.

Ted rose before she could act. "Finish your breakfast."

"I should—"

"Keep your ass in that chair. This is the kind of job made for an overprotective father." He winked. "I met enough angry daddies in my youth to know what to say."

As Ted neared the twins, he heard the man spouting a line of bullshit. "...modeling opportunities for beautiful ladies."

Fucking perv. Ted didn't smile as the guy noticed his approach. As soon as he neared, Lin tucked close to his side. "Hi, Daddy." She smiled up at him.

"Hey, baby girl." He put a hand on Mae's shoulder and found her stiff. "Everything okay?"

"This man wants to take our picture."

"Oh, he does, does he?" Ted eyed the man, whose pale skin sweated.

"You must be the twins' dad. I was just telling them about my photography business. Always looking for new talent. Your daughters are quite beautiful."

"I know. However, we've chosen to focus more on what's inside than outside, especially given their impressionable age. Girls, why don't you bring Mom that bacon. She was just saying she was craving more." He waited until they were out of earshot before smiling and saying in a deadly tone, "Listen, you pervy fucking bastard, and listen good. Stay away from my daughters, or you'll be one of those unfortunate souls who falls off the ship at sea and is never found again."

The fellow's eyes widened. "Is that a threat?"

"A promise. Don't come near my girls." Damn, there

was something awesome about calling them his. About taking on a role he'd never even considered.

The other fellow, too cocky by far, sneered. "We both know they're not yours. Or your wife's. Was it your idea to adopt Oriental? In-home dining rather than takeout."

If they'd been anywhere else, Ted would have decked him. But he couldn't get tossed off the ship. It took iron control to murmur, "Say one more word, and you won't live to see the sunset."

"You can't threaten me," the man blustered.

Crash. Joanna accidentally bumped into the fellow, sending him reeling into the buffet.

"Oops. Sorry about that. Clumsy me," she exclaimed without a hint of apology.

When the perv would have whirled from the mess to freak on Joanna, she subtly hooked his ankle, sending him crashing to the deck.

"You fucking bitch. How dare you touch me?"

"I dare because those are my nieces, asshole," she said, leaning down so that only Ted and the perv could hear.

"You'll pay for this," threatened the man as the ship's staff came running.

Joanna pointed at the perv. "That man touched me without my permission."

"Did not!"

When the staff looked at Ted, he nodded. "And he tried to get my daughters to go somewhere private with him. You might want to check his camera."

The very idea led to the perv being taken away with

Joanna following behind, threatening to sue if he and his wandering hands weren't put ashore.

Ted returned to the table and the girls, who sat quietly with their mother. She wore a bemused expression, but Mae nodded at him as if she approved, while Lin beamed. "Way to go, Daddy. Can we go for a swim now?"

"Only after we have our lessons." Because he wanted the girls able to defend themselves should the next perv be a little more handsy.

After forty-five minutes of sweating, the swim in the pool refreshed. After a light lunch, the ship docked. The family group, minus Joanna, who'd disappeared again, set off to explore. They headed on foot into the town, the bazaar-type atmosphere loud and bright. Great to hide in, but not so good for keeping an eye out for suspicious sorts.

Logically, he knew Ronin and his cronies couldn't have found them, and yet, Macey's paranoia proved contagious. Especially after his run-in with the perv that morning. The nerve of that fucker, soliciting the girls right in front of him.

What would have happened if he or Macey hadn't been around? The girls were smart enough to not go off with a stranger, but what if the guy threatened? He really needed to work on those self-defense lessons with them.

The girls browsed a selection of shell art. He leaned close to Macey and muttered, "Is it me, or is being a parent stressful?"

She side-eyed him. "What makes you say that?"

"There are so many dangers they're unaware of, and a parent's job is to keep them safe."

"Mine never did," was her low reply.

"Mine either." He shoved his hands into his pockets. "I kind of wish I'd had someone looking out for me, though. It would have made things easier."

"But then you wouldn't be the person you are today," she remarked.

"Exactly." He grimaced. "I've not been a model example."

"Dwelling on our past mistakes doesn't help us move forward."

"Helps to make sure I don't repeat them, though."

"Ain't that the truth?" she said on a sigh, following as the girls flitted off and pointed as they identified the array of spices being hung and dried in a stall.

"You never got involved with anyone after your ex," he stated.

"Who told you that?" she asked, only to groan. "The girls."

"They're under the impression that you're pining for their father."

She grimaced. "More like never repeating that mistake. Even now, I can't believe I let someone control me like that."

"It's hard to recognize the signs of an unhealthy relationship, especially when we're young. It doesn't help that the toxic ones tend to be the hardest to shake."

"Speaking from experience?"

"Not with women, if that's what you're asking."

He noted the blush as she quickly exhaled. "No. I didn't mean— Just—" she stammered.

Ted laughed. "My toxicity was with drugs and alcohol. I knew they were bad for me. Hated how they made me feel, but it took me a while to break away. And even now, I'm constantly on guard."

"Always worried you'll get caught in that trap again." She cocked her head as she eyed him. "I guess we're both living with ghosts."

"Can you imagine what life would be like if they stopped haunting us?"

Her expression took on a sad mien. "No, I can't."

His turn to grab her hand and hold it. She glanced down at their laced fingers and him. For a moment, he thought she'd pull away. Instead, she leaned closer to him.

"Nine o'clock."

"What?" It took him a second to grasp that she wanted him looking in a specific direction. He shifted to subtly peer.

Someone was taking pictures of the crowd. Probably to post on social media. Moving quickly, he tucked his arm around Macey and tilted them to shield the girls. It wouldn't do to have their faces plastered anywhere. Recognition software might suss them out.

"We should get out of here," she muttered. "According to my messages from Mother, the first house to look at is past downtown, we can walk there."

"I'll wrangle the girls." By wrangle, he meant take them each by the hand and begin walking. Lin followed, but Mae dug in her heels. She tugged to free herself, but he held tightly.

"What are you doing? I'm not a baby."

"Just making sure you don't get kidnapped."

"No one is going to abduct us," was her disdainful reply.

"Hate to break it to you, protected princess, but every day, dozens of kids, probably more like hundreds, are taken against their will."

"Why?" Lin asked with an innocence he didn't want to ruin.

But Mae, who might be the same age, but appeared more street-savvy, knew. "He's talking about human trafficking."

"Only bad people do that, and we stay away from them."

"Because bad people wear a sign around their neck?" he mocked. Probably not the mature thing to do, but the twins had a cockiness about them that would get them into trouble.

"Of course not, but we're careful," Mae insisted.

"So careful you got caught up talking with a man this morning at breakfast when you should have walked away?" Macey declared as they cleared the crush of people.

"We didn't want to be rude. We weren't going to go anywhere with him."

"You have to be more cautious. There are bad people out there who would do you harm."

"You just want us to be paranoid like you," Mae hotly

declared, tearing free from his grip so she could confront her mother.

"It's called staying safe," Macey said primly.

"No, it's not. You're afraid of something," Mae stated.

"Don't be silly."

"Then you're okay if I call Pedro from school and let him know we're okay? He's probably worried and all, given that our house burned down." Lin was the one to provide the sly request.

"And what about the police? I'm sure they want to talk to us. Arson is a crime."

Ted saw the trap the girls laid, with no way for Macey to escape it. He jumped in and threw himself on the grenade to save her.

"You can't call anyone. Because no one can know we're together."

"Why not?" Mae's gaze slewed in his direction.

He needed an excuse. One good enough to keep the girls from questioning the subterfuge. One that would take the focus off Macey and put it on him.

He blurted the first thing that came to mind. "I think it was my ex-wife who burned down my dojo and your house. If she finds out I'm on this cruise with your mom, who knows what she'll do. I'm afraid she'll come after us."

13

RONIN

RONIN FLEW to the United States the moment it was confirmed.

Macey lived. As did his daughters. Very intelligent girls, according to school records. It was via their classmates that he got the most details and a picture. Serious-looking, and most definitely his.

Macey had much to answer for.

By now, Macey probably suspected that Ronin was coming after her. He'd not been exactly subtle when he set fire to all the places connected to her and his daughters. Let her fear his wrath. Let her lie awake at night and worry. Twitch at every shadow.

She deserved it for what she'd put him through. She'd pay, once he found her.

Which was proving more difficult than expected. It would seem that Macey had a knack for disappearing. And she'd once more vanished. However, unlike a decade ago, when he thought she'd died, this time, he actively sought her. She could try and hide, but he wouldn't stop looking.

Given that he couldn't exactly sit on his hands and patiently wait, he'd flown to the States, and was now in the penthouse condo he owned in San Francisco. Someone had kindly fetched Ralph, the last person to have seen Macey.

A man who was proving disappointing in the information department.

"Let's start over," he said, pulling the gag from Ralph's mouth.

"I don't know anything else. I swear."

Ronin glanced at Jiao, his current right-hand man, the newest in a long line of disappointments since Chen. Some days, he regretted not killing his old friend. Other days, he thought about bringing him back. But then he would appear weak.

That wasn't something he ever allowed.

"I think our guest needs softening." A statement that led to Jiao hefting a hammer.

Ralph squeak and began pleading. They always did. Ronin had long ago learned to tune it out.

Once the screams tapered to moans and sobbing, Ronin stepped close and pressed his fingers into a wound pierced by bone.

Ralph blubbered. "I don't know."

Ronin believed him. But his frustration demanded some kind of satisfaction.

His phone went off, a standard ring because he couldn't stand all the ridiculous sounds other people chose for theirs. There was nothing wrong with being traditional.

Lee, his manservant, held it up. "Kira calling, sir."

"I'll take it." Wiping his bloody fingers on a rag, Ronin then took the outstretched phone. "You'd better have news."

"I do."

"Give me a second." Ronin cast a glance at Jiao. "Dispose of him."

Ralph roused enough to moan and beg, "No, please."

Ignoring the plea, Ronin stepped out of the concrete bunker—with walls so thick, no one could hear the screams. Built as a panic room in the center of the condo, it served as a place to handle delicate matters. The drain in the floor had been added in after the fact.

Only once he'd entered his office and closed the door did he speak again. "What did you find out?"

"Not much yet. Whoever is helping her, hid her tracks pretty damned good. Every electronic record is gone or changed."

"But you did find something."

"I think I've located your daughters."

His body went still, and his tone low. "Are you sure?"

"Like ninety percent certain it's them."

"And how did you arrive at this premise?"

"Using the images we retrieved, we've been scanning social media." While Macey might have tried to keep her social media presence to virtually nothing, she'd been less successful with curbing that of his daughters. He had many images of them, indulging in serious pursuits of which he approved. At least Macey appeared to be giving them a proper education. However, they needed their father.

"I take it you got a hit."

"The facial recognition software has been filtering every video feed and online platform out there. Which takes time, I should add. But we got a possible match."

His phone dinged, and he held it away from his ear to see the incoming image. It showed a cruise ship with people at the rails, waving. Too small to tell much. He had the picture mirror on the screen that hung on his wall. He stepped close to it and scanned the many faces.

"You better not have called me on a maybe." His eyes quickly stroked left and right before pausing. There, at the top, a pair of girls with pink and cream hats, standing between a woman and a man. He zoomed in and would admit to being impressed that the software had picked up on their faces. High-quality images made things so much easier when it came to surveillance.

"Given we were concerned that the image was a false positive, I contacted a passenger aboard the ship and got them to locate the children and send me more pictures. It's a match."

"You found them." Triumph filled him. One step closer to getting his revenge. "What of their mother?" What of his disobedient wife?

"They are traveling with a woman who appears to be Macey, though she isn't quite lining up with your pictures. It's possible she's had some facial surgery. She appears to be traveling with Mr. Grady, who changed his name to Hogan, and some woman on the manifest posing as an aunt."

The news that his wife remained with that man, that ex-soldier running a sham studio, burned.

"Excellent work, Kira. Have your informant monitor my daughters and their mother until I can make arrangements for their retrieval."

"Unfortunately, my eyes and ears on board have been removed from the ship. But I am working on finding a new passenger or crewmember to use."

Ronin cut her off. "Don't bother. Send me the itinerary. I'll handle the rescue of my family from here on out."

He might even go in person so he could hear Macey grovel.

And then he'd show his daughters what he did to those who betrayed him. It would serve as their first lesson in how to please their father.

CHAPTER FOURTEEN

PORTIA WAITED until they'd exited the first house, with its traffic noise and neighbors with the many barking dogs to lay into Ted. The girls had skipped ahead, intrigued when Portia had mentioned perhaps sticking around the Caribbean for a while. Getting them some tutors. It both pleased and worried her to hear children excited about a possible one-on-one education.

As they pointed out the lovely shrubs lining the road on their way back to the ship, she hissed. "What the heck were you thinking? Previously married with a crazy ex-wife? *That* was your best lie?"

He rolled his shoulders. "I panicked. Said the first thing I could think of they might consider a good enough secret. You know, you could say thank you. The only reason I had to lie was because you haven't told them the truth."

Her lips thinned. "Do you really think now is the time?"

"Yes. Or has it not occurred to you that if your ex

knows you're alive, he might, let's say, manage to find them? What if he shows up and says, '*Hey, I'm your daddy. Wanna come live with me since your mean mommy tried to keep us apart?*'"

"The girls would never..." She bit her lip. Portia honestly had no idea how they'd react.

"If your ex is as good a manipulator as you claim, then he'd have no problem weaving some fairy tale where you're the villain. And before you say that wouldn't happen, let me add that I've seen it in action."

"I'll just make sure he never finds them."

"You're being stupid," he said bluntly.

"No, I'm a coward," she admitted, seeing the girls had stopped by a vendor selling deep-fried pastries. "Telling them the truth is going to hurt them. It's going to affect everything." Especially their trust in their mother. She'd known that for a while. Kept her head in the sand, hoping she'd never have to deal with it, and yet, lived in daily fear that the truth would come out.

"You're their mother. They'll forgive you."

"Will they?" They were part of the reason that Ronin still lived. She couldn't kill their father.

The girls each got a hot pastry rolled in sugar. Since they still had time before they had to board, they walked the beach, the girls kicking at the waves as they ate their sweet treats. Portia hadn't gotten one for herself, but Ted had splurged for a three-scoop ice cream cone.

She'd said no, but eyeing the melting, cold and creamy goodness, she regretted the decision.

"Want a bite?" he offered, having noticed her hungry stare.

She should say no. It was pure sugar. He'd licked it already.

Hmm. That wasn't a deterrent, actually. She reached for it, wrapping her hand around his to draw it to her mouth.

She took a long lick, conscious that he watched, his gaze smoldering.

"My turn." He angled it to bite at the section she'd just licked, holding her gaze the entire time.

Her next taste was openmouthed, over the top. She was pretty sure she heard him groan.

His free hand curled around her waist and drew her nearer. Part of the act, or did he feel the heat between them, too?

Was it just because it had been so long? Did she imagine the passion simmering within him? The ice cream stood between them, neither of them eating it, their gazes locked. What would happen if she kissed him?

If—

"Aaaawww!" The sharp shriek doused her with cold reality.

"Lin!" She shouted her daughter's name as she whirled, her hand sliding into her pocket to the slit that gave her access to a small pistol. She lunged forward, ready to sprint, only to find herself grinding to a halt. She glared at the fingers hooked in the waistband of her shorts.

"Let go," she growled.

"Don't you dare pull that gun. The girls are fine."

"But Lin..." Screeched again as a wave rolled onto the

beach, and something slimy touched Lin's ankle. Which led to Mae mocking her.

There was no danger, and yet Portia had almost pulled a gun in public. That wouldn't have ended well.

"We need to go back to the ship." At least, she did. Because Mae was right. Paranoia was ruling her decisions. And if she wasn't careful, it would ruin their lives. "Can you watch them? I need to freshen up."

She went ahead, but it wasn't long before the girls joined her, Ted bringing up the rear. Small hands slipped into hers as they skipped.

"Why so sad, Mommy?" Lin asked.

"Not sad. Just tired and hot." Her wan smile probably helped with that lie.

"Your mom just needs a good night's sleep, I think."

"Can we have dinner in our room tonight?" Mae asked. "We're tired, too."

Portia shook her head. "You're just saying that because of me. We'll go to dinner, and whatever tonight's entertainment is."

"Actually," Mae said, "we were kind of hoping to go star watching tonight. We found out that we can borrow a telescope, and there's supposed to be a meteor shower."

"I guess I can—"

Mae interrupted. "Aunt Joanna already said she'd take us if it's okay with you."

"Can we?" Lin exclaimed, bouncing ahead and clasping her hands.

Portia's first impulse was to utter a resounding "*no*," but with what excuse? Joanna could watch over the girls.

She was tired. And this was exactly the type of thing the girls enjoyed.

"Fine. But straight to your room after."

"Yes, Mother. We'll be sure to be quiet too so we don't wake you or Daddy."

There was nothing else to say, and she was quite relieved to find out that the man who'd talked to them that morning at breakfast had been put ashore. They'd be fine.

Still, as she paced the room, Ted couldn't help but remark, "Helicopter much?"

"What?"

"Hover. Suffocate. Panic over everything."

She scowled. "You wouldn't understand. You're not a parent."

"No, I'm not. But look at you. What do you really think can happen on a ship?"

"Would you like a list?" Because she had plenty of suggestions.

"How many of the items on it are realistic?"

"The danger that my girls are in isn't run-of-the-mill."

"No, but at the same time, be careful that your protective actions don't become worse than the thing you're protecting them from."

"Are you implying that I'm as bad as Ronin?"

"No. But you are a tiger."

She knew exactly in what context he meant it, and she wasn't ashamed. Not one bit. "Damned straight, I'm a tiger. Which is worse than a soccer mom or a bear mom. I know I take paranoia to a new level. I'm a doctor, I've seen some of the worst things out there," she huffed. "I am fully aware that I'm crazy, but you know I do it to keep them safe."

"You can't turn them into prisoners while doing so."

"They're free..." She trailed off. Free to do what exactly? She'd torn them from their lives. Forbidden them from having any contact with it. Would be turning them into new people. She couldn't give them a choice. The cage she'd put them in didn't have visible bars.

"It doesn't have to be this difficult. Talk to them. Explain everything."

"They'll hate me." She suddenly collapsed in on herself, her ass hitting the edge of the bed, her shoulders rounding with defeat. "They won't understand, and I can't stop myself from acting like this. They're all I have, and I'm afraid I'll lose them."

She leaned forward, her face buried in her hands. The bed dipped as he sat beside her. His arm stretched around her in a hug. She leaned into him.

"I can't imagine what it's like living like that," he said softly.

"You have nightmares when you sleep. Mine happen when I'm awake."

"And those are even more terrifying." Said in a low rumble. "They are why I used to do the drugs and drink. I'd see a face and be reminded. A noise would set me off."

"How do you stop it?"

"You don't. It will always be there to a certain extent. It's how you handle it that makes a difference."

"Your nightmares are about things you did in the past, though. For me, it's about what could still happen while Ronin is out there."

"The worst thing being...what?"

She blinked at him. "I'd say that's obvious. Him taking the girls."

"I would have said killing you."

She shook her head. "My life means nothing if it keeps them safe. But the thought of him having his daughters, of him being able to influence them, maybe even hurt them..." She shook her head.

"Meaning you won't ever relax until he's dead."

"What if that's worse?" She glanced at the fingers clasped in her lap as she kept silent about her other fear.

What if Ronin died because of her? And she lived with the guilt of having killed the twins' father. Or worse, what if the girls found out what she'd done, and she lost them forever?

CHAPTER FIFTEEN

HER SHOULDERS SHOOK, and he didn't know what to do. Macey had hit her rock bottom, and now she couldn't see a way out.

There were no words Ted could really use to help. No magical cure. The thing about terror was that it wasn't always rational. But it certainly was pervasive.

Ted had only meant to try and relax her, his fingers kneading the flesh of her shoulders, digging into the knots that kept her tense.

As she relaxed, she moaned, and her head fell back, exposing the smooth column of her throat. He couldn't help but kiss it. She shivered, and her lips parted.

Had she told him to stop, he would have. Probably would have left the room and swum laps until he collapsed. But instead, she turned and cupped his face, drawing his mouth to hers.

Asking for a kiss.

She got a storm.

His passion, barely leashed, spilled forth, and he

kissed her back, hard, demanding. She replied in kind, her breath hot. He ended up sitting on the couch with her in his lap, making out. His hands roamed her body, and she leaned away from him so he could strip her shirt, leaving her clad in only a bra on top.

He buried his face in her cleavage, but that wasn't enough. He slid to the side so she sat on the couch, and then he knelt on the floor. He tugged at her shorts, pulling them down over her legs. The holster with her gun was strapped to her thigh, and his fingers might have trembled a bit as he undid the clasp. He lay it within arm's reach, her gaze following its path.

"Relax," he whispered.

"I don't know how." Spoken as she sat in her underwear, beautiful, her eyes at half-mast, her lips full and pouty.

"Then let me help you."

His hands cupped her hips and drew her forward on the couch so she sat on the edge. He placed a kiss between her breasts, then lower, on her upper belly. Then lower still. Macey trembled with desire. He could smell her through the thin fabric of her panties as arousal moistened her cleft. He used his teeth to tug, and when that didn't work so well, his hands made quick work of the material in his way.

He pressed his face against her mound and nipped, a signal for her to part her legs. Her sex gleamed, pink and wet. Tasty, he'd wager. He blew softly, and her sex quivered. Next, the wet tip of his tongue traced the edges of her lips, the feathery touch drawing a moan.

The sound emboldened him, and he gripped her hips

tighter, drawing her to his mouth. He licked her slit, a long, wet stroke of his tongue that had her moaning again.

Then, as if shocked by the noise, she shoved a fist into her mouth. But she didn't ask him to stop, so he licked her again, and again, delving between her lips, thrusting his tongue into her pussy. Macey clutched the couch cushions, her hips thrusting slightly as she met the cadence that he set.

At times, her thighs turned into tight vises around his head. As if he cared. He teased her and tasted. Flicked his tongue against her clit and almost got whiplash as she bucked. He grabbed hold of her clit with his lips and sucked on her sensitive flesh.

She trembled and uttered a low moan that vibrated past the fist in her mouth. When her orgasm hit, he caught it, and then kept stroking it, leaving her panting for more.

She shoved at him, and he thought: *this is it, we're done*.

But his ass hit the floor, and then she hit him as she dove on top of him, her hands tugging at his shirt. He helped her strip it from his body, exposing his hard form. His turn to tremble as she stroked a hand down his chest to the waistband of his pants.

He couldn't remove them while sitting, so he stood, and had the pleasure of looking down to see her on her knees, tugging at them. Exposing him in all his erect glory. She reached out and grabbed him, drawing a hiss.

His hips thrust.

She laughed. "My turn."

"Maybe later." Because if she kept touching him, he'd

spill, and then he wouldn't know the pleasure of sinking into her body.

He drew her to her feet and against him, his cock trapped between their bodies, but he reveled in the skin-to-skin contact. His lips latched on to hers, and she opened to him, their tongues, breath, and passion entwining.

Her nipples pebbled against his chest, berries he suddenly had to taste. Ted leaned her far enough back that he could bend and take one into his mouth.

Macey moaned and bucked her pelvis as his tongue swirled around the tip. He thrust a thigh between her legs, and she rode it, rubbing her wet cleft against him, drawing a pleased growl.

She was everything he ever wanted in a woman. Passionate. Sweet. Responsive to his touch.

His.

He wanted to join with her. To feel her surrounding him. He turned so he could once more sit on the couch, but he drew her down with him, getting her to straddle his lap, his cock trapped under her cleft.

She rocked against him, teasing him with the heat of her core, lubing him with her cream. She lifted herself enough that his cock bobbed upright. The head of his prick rubbed the entrance to her sex. She wiggled a bit, teasing.

His fingers dug into her hips as he resisted the instinct to slam into her.

He didn't want to go too fast, but he might just die if—

She sat down, and he gasped as the heat of her surrounded him. Pulsed. Clenched him tightly.

"Oh, that's nice," she murmured.

"Nice?" he grumbled.

"Perfect," she amended as she began rocking atop him. It took an already pleasurable sensation and multiplied it by infinity. He fit her snugly, his cock buried to the hilt, her pussy squeezing. Her breath hot and panting.

Together, they moved in rhythm, his hands on her waist, his hips doing their best to grind while she rocked.

He didn't need to feel the tension in her body to know that she was about to come again. On his cock.

Her breathing turned ragged. Her nails dug into his shoulders as the pleasure coiled inside her.

At the moment of climax, she opened her eyes, and their gazes locked.

Ted knew he couldn't yell his pleasure, and the fact that he couldn't made it more intense. He bucked, his hips thrusting up, deep.

Hard...

She came even harder.

Then collapsed against him.

He carried her to bed, where they spooned and talked softly. Of nothing and everything. It led to them making love a second time, with him sliding into her from behind, and falling asleep spooned.

There were no nightmares that night. Nothing but trust and comfort and blushes in the morning as a knock came from the door.

"Hey, I think you locked us out," Lin yelled through the door.

A good thing they'd locked it from their side. It gave them time to dress before they faced the girls and Joanna's knowing smirk.

But the best part of all, the pink blush in Macey's cheeks every time she looked at him.

CHAPTER SIXTEEN

THEY SPENT the day at sea, picking and choosing what activities they wanted to participate in. As a family.

It was beyond strange as Portia got to indulge in what having a man around could be like. Ted catered to her, bringing her fruity, iced drinks, no alcohol, respecting the fact that she wasn't a drinker. A good number of people had a tendency to be pushy when they found out that she preferred to remain completely sober. Insisted it was just one drink. It wouldn't hurt.

Maybe not, but Portia preferred to be in complete control at all times.

What she didn't say no to was the ridiculously delicious treats Ted also managed to scrounge. Skewers of shrimp with a sweet and spicy dipping sauce. Chocolate-covered grapes. Even bacon-wrapped chicken bites.

He fed some pieces to her, his eyes twinkling with mirth, his lips curved.

"I can feed myself," she'd protested.

"Got to make people believe we're a couple. Wife."
He winked.

"Whatever you say, pookie." She gasped and felt her
cheeks burn when he dropped a light kiss on her mouth.
She flamed to life when he rubbed lotion onto her back.

She made an excuse, and he quickly followed. They
practically ran to the room and never made it to the bed.
He took her against the closed door, thrusting into her
while she clung to him, gasping. Coming. Hugged him as
their breathing slowed, then raced back before anyone
noticed they were gone together for too long.

She went for a swim to sluice her body—the tepid
pool water could have used some ice.

The whole day could be described only as amazing.

Not just for her. Portia wasn't the only one who got to
enjoy Ted, having him attentive to their needs. The girls
benefitted, too. He brought them fresh-cut fruit with
whipped cream for dipping. Iced tea with fancy
umbrellas that the girls claimed were an ecologically
unsound and decorative waste, and yet, she noticed they
kept them and wore them tucked into their hair.

The twins liked Ted. For the first time in a long
while, they weren't glued to their tablets, or with their
faces buried in a book, ignoring the world around them.
They were swimming and practicing their martial arts
moves—at least Lin was. Mae had started the day doing
stuff with them, but as the hours went by, she became
withdrawn. Kept asking to go lie down in her room.

"Are you sick?"

Mae shook her head. Still, more than a few times,
Portia felt her forehead. Kept asking, "Does your stomach

hurt?" She went through a list of possible ailments, trying to figure out what might be wrong with Mae.

In the end, she could only surmise. "I think you got too much sun."

"Yup. I bet that's what's wrong." Mae nodded. "Meaning, I should go to bed early and skip the show."

"I'll pass on it as well and stay with you." Guilt filled her that she'd not noticed Mae taxing herself in the sun. In her defense, Lin had spent much more time and appeared fine. Yet Portia had to remind herself, that being twins didn't mean her daughters would react the same. Something was wrong with Mae, and Portia wasn't about to leave her.

"You can't stay," Mae blurted. "You should go. Take Lin and Ted with you. Aunt Joanna, too."

"I am not leaving you alone." She knew that heat exhaustion could lead to a fever as the body overheated, then to vomiting. Never mind that Mae didn't seem that bad-off or have any of those symptoms. What if the reaction was delayed?

"I'm not a baby, Mom. I'm not sick. Just tired. Let me go to sleep. Alone," she added firmly.

Portia didn't like this obstinance. "No. You're only ten. Meaning, by law, you require supervision."

"Okay, boomer." Said with a roll of her eyes.

"Excuse me?"

"I said, okay, boomer. It's a newish slang expression meaning you're old."

"As in Baby Boomer old?" Portia blinked. "I'm not even thirty-five. Boomers were born in the forties to sixties."

"You're being clingy. I might be ten in Earth rotations, but mentally, we both know I'm much older. And let's be honest, isn't that the age we should really be focusing on?"

Exquisite argument, and if this were a debate, she might win. But Portia was a mom. And she didn't negotiate. "You know what, I will go to the show with your sister and Ted, but your aunt will be sticking around."

Mae opened her mouth to protest.

"She's staying, and that's final. But she'll be in the other room, with the door open so she can hear if you need her."

Fine. Treat me like a baby." Mae sulked, not looking sick at all, more like a prelude to the sullen teenager getting ready to burst free.

Portia didn't care. In this case, it wasn't age that was really the factor, it was her caution. She'd talked to Mother that day, and Tanya had been texting, too.

Ronin had left China. His plane was sitting in San Francisco...but no one appeared able to lay eyes on him.

Where was he?

It was no coincidence that Ronin had come to the United States for a visit. He'd be looking for them. This might be the last trip, heck, the last *day* they had before all hell broke loose.

Lin wanted to go to the show. Mae didn't. If trouble struck, Joanna could handle one girl easily enough, and Portia would have the other.

But she couldn't tell Mae that Joanna was to be her bodyguard. She leaned in and kissed her forehead. "Feel better. I'll see you in the morning."

Nothing happened. Lin sat between them at the show, exclaiming over the bright outfits and the dancing. Every so often, Portia would glance over her daughter's head and see Ted watching her. Smiling. It made her feel warm inside.

After the performance, they took a stroll on the deck. Hand in hand as Lin chattered ahead of them, more child than scholar for once. A few times, Lin glanced at them, noticing their clasped digits. She wore a smile each time.

Then again, so did Portia. Returning to their cabin, they entered the master part of the suite to find Joanna snoring on the couch. She tiptoed into the other room to see Mae sleeping on her side. A quick touch of her forehead showed it normal temperature. She brushed a few strands of hair from her daughter's cheek before she kissed it. Then she kissed Lin as she tucked her in. Something she'd gotten out of the habit doing because the girls had begun scoffing at the practice.

Too bad. Portia wasn't ready to let them grow up yet.

Joanna staggered from the couch to her bed with the girls. The door between the rooms closed. A moment later, she was in Ted's arms. Their first tumble into bed was hot and fast, her lips sucking at the flesh of his shoulder as the orgasm took her, and she fought not to scream.

Their second bout of lovemaking was slow as they lay on their sides, spooned. He slid into her, and his rhythm was more a deep rocking. Soft and sensual. When she came, she sighed his name. "Ted."

He also groaned hers against her nape as he remained inside her. "Macey."

She froze. He'd done it again. The third time now since the trip had started. In vulnerable moments, he slipped and called her by her old name rather than her new one. But she didn't have the heart to chastise him. What did it matter? In a few days, they'd have to go their separate ways. Her to a new life, a new identity. Him to... somewhere else. Where she wouldn't see him. There wasn't really a choice. Until she dealt with Ronin, she couldn't get involved with anyone.

But the only way to handle Ronin was to kill him.

Kill the father of her girls.

Why did she struggle with it? The man was a monster. One she'd once loved.

The next day, the ship docked bright and early. A shower with Ted left her feeling energized. However, the same could not be said of her daughters.

"What's wrong?" she asked when she peeked in and saw them both abed.

Joanna finished lacing her shoes. "Not feeling too good. Neither am I. I was going to see if I could find something to settle our tummies."

"Oh, no." Concern filled Portia as she sat on the side of the bed and did her mom thing with the hand on the forehead.

"It's my stomach that aches, not my head," Lin said with a roll of her eyes.

"We probably have to poop," Mae stated all too seriously.

Which made Lin giggle. "Do not."

"Do, too." Firmly said. Mae then turned her gaze to

Portia. "I'm going to stay close to a bathroom today, if that's okay."

"Me, too!" Lin chimed in.

"All right. I can get some work done."

"You are not staying with us," Mae declared.

"If you're not feeling well—"

"If you stay, then Ted stays."

"Probably."

"He can't. What if we do have to poop. Like urgently." Lin's eyes widened. "He might smell it."

Which having once been a young girl herself was understandably horrifying. Even now...Portia might be sharing a room with Ted, but she'd been doing any number twos in the girls' bathroom. Being a scientist who knew how the body worked didn't mean she wanted the man she was sleeping with to know she didn't always smell pretty.

"I could tell him to leave."

"Oh my God. Just go with him," Mae exclaimed. "Why must you be so clingy?"

The rebuke stung. They didn't understand what she did to protect them. Maybe she should take Ted's advice and tell them. Tell them while they were sick? Later. "Tell you what, if Joanna doesn't mind sticking around, then I'll go and take Ted with me." Mother had lined up two more houses for her to look at. Although, if the girls couldn't handle the heat, then maybe life in the Caribbean wasn't for them.

She wondered where Ted planned to move.

Joanna returned with a mini pharmacy of stomach

remedies. "Aunt Jo, tell Mom she should go do the tourist thing with Ted."

"Go do the tourist thing," Joanna parroted. "I'll hang with the hooligans."

"Are you sure?" she asked.

"Yes, I'm sure," Joanna exclaimed. She handed the bag to the girls. "Read the instructions and figure out what dosage we need to take." She practically shoved Portia into the other room and shut the door. "You need to stop acting crazy."

"I am not acting crazy. I'm their mother. I want to make sure they're okay."

"They're fine. I don't even think they're sick."

"Why would they lie?"

Joanna snorted. "Are you really that dense?"

"Apparently, so why don't you explain it to me?"

"They're trying to give you and Ted some alone time."

She blinked. "Why?"

"Why do you think, idiot? They like him, and they obviously think it's time their mom stopped being alone and found someone to love."

"I don't love him."

"Maybe not yet, but he makes you happy. And they see that. Is it any wonder they're conspiring to have you go out and have a day of fun with your man?"

"Shhh," she hissed. She glanced at the closed bathroom door. "He is not my man."

"He could be."

"You know why I can't get involved with anyone. Ronin—"

"Has been out of your life for ten years. And, hopefully, that will last ten more."

"Doubtful. He knows I'm alive."

"Or so we assume. What if he wasn't the one who burned down your house? Could be Chen had friends, or a lover who decided to retaliate. It might not have been him."

"Then why else would he come to the US?" she countered.

"Business. It wouldn't be the first time. And for your information, he's gone now."

"What?"

"Did you not read Mother's latest report?"

Portia shook her head. She'd not had time yet.

"Ronin's plane went back to China, and he's been spotted there."

"That doesn't mean he's not looking for us. He—"

"Would you stop it with the excuses." Joanna grabbed her by the upper arms and gave her a little shake. "Don't be me and miss out on life. Embrace every chance at happiness while you can."

Portia might have replied, but Ted emerged, hair still slick, jaw freshly trimmed. Looking delicious, especially as he said, "I'm famished. Ready to eat?"

She was ready for all kinds of things with him.

They spent an idyllic time, hand in hand, visiting an old fort, playing the part of tourist. Having lunch at a cute open-air bistro on the beach. Playing the honeymooning couple who were thinking of renting in the islands and relocating.

She'd called Joanna a few times to check on the girls.

Fine. Reading on their tablets. Relaxing. The midafternoon check-in text didn't receive a reply.

Could be Joanna was busy. She waited even as she aimed their steps in the direction of the ship. Fifteen minutes later, she texted again, and when she still didn't get a reply, she called.

It went to voicemail, and her pace turned into a jog.

"What's wrong?" Ted asked, keeping up.

"Joanna's not answering." Which was bad. So bad. She could feel it in her gut.

"Could be she has a good reason." Said even as he lengthened his stride.

"Could be." But Portia knew. She just knew something awful had happened. Punishment because she'd dared to put her selfish needs in front of that of her kids.

The cruise ship appeared the same as they'd left it. Not on fire, which had been one of her fears. No local constabulary appeared to be interested in it.

A few early returnees straggled up the gangplank to the ship, carrying large tote bags crammed with local artisanal treasures. Conscious that she might be watched, Portia marched quickly, doing her best to appear calm. Ted didn't fare any better, his expression grim as they moved onto the ship then quickly to their level and hall. Rather than enter her room, she used her passkey to go into the one the girls and Joanna shared.

The latter was snoring on a bed. But the twins...the twins were gone.

17

THE TWINS

SITTING IN THE PIZZA SHOP, Mae made a point of not fidgeting as much as her sister. This was, after all, her idea. Lin just came along because Mae told her to.

Her sister kept casting worried glances around. "I don't know if this is a good idea. Mom will be worried if she gets back to the ship early and can't find us."

"Mom is worried all the time," Mae replied. Even more since they'd left to come on the cruise. Something had happened. Something that necessitated them leaving in the middle of the night. Because she didn't, for one minute, believe that fake story Mom had put out about Ted winning some contest. Nor did she buy that Ted hid from an ex-wife.

By now, her observations had led her to believe that Ted acted as some kind of bodyguard. It would explain his gun. She'd seen it by accident, tucked in his suitcase. Bigger than the one her mom carried around.

They were spooked, and it had to do with Mae's dad. A father who wasn't dead.

Lin was the one who had overheard everything the first day on the ship. She'd immediately told Mae.

Funny how their mother worried that Mae and Lin weren't like other kids. Yet in one respect, they certainly were. They'd both always wanted to meet their father.

Knowing their dad existed and hadn't died, that their mother never wanted them to meet him, that she'd lied? It was the ultimate betrayal.

Once Mae knew that he existed, she'd decided that she had to meet the man who'd given them half their DNA. The problem was finding him. As it turned out, their mother hadn't even given them his real name. Or hers, for that matter. Mae had always known her as Portia, although her friends, those whom she called *aunt*, sometimes referred to her as Tiger.

But Ted knew her as Macey. Macey who? Knowing their mom had gone to school with Ted didn't make it easy to find. There were no public records with that name.

Nothing at all. It was as if their mother hadn't existed in the past. Or she'd been wiped clean.

Which led to Mae looking for her father. Not easy given all she had to go on was a possible first name: Ronin. More than ten million results popped up when she searched. Adding Asian to it on a wild guess given her obvious heritage didn't reduce it by much.

She needed a way to fine-tune the results. On a lark, she'd done a search on Macey and Ronin. Not expecting much, only a zillion more useless hits.

Bingo.

The very first thing to pop up was a blurb in Chinese,

which she'd taught herself to read at the age of eight. Meaning, she could tell it was a marriage announcement. From over a decade ago. Could it be possible? She hardly dared to believe it. And yet when she loaded the tiny article with its corresponding image, there was no mistaking the face. However, the hair was much lighter in color. It was Mom, her nose not quite the same, and her chin now wider, less pointed. But still her.

Standing beside her, solemn-faced, was a man with Asian features. Mae and Lin's father.

"He is handsome," Lin said when Mae showed her what she'd found. Silly Mother, thinking the parental controls she'd enabled would keep Mae off the Wi-Fi. The hardest part was finding excuses to leave her family so she could have some privacy to do her searching. She'd finally had to fake being sick to get some uninterrupted time.

It had paid off.

While Joanna had snored, ensconced in the bathroom with the door closed, and the fan running, Mae had filled Lin in on what she'd found. "There aren't too many pictures of him, but it doesn't look like he's changed much. And he's rich. Some kind of businessman." Mae had been digging, looking for every nugget of information she could find.

"Do we have other siblings?" Lin had asked, perched on the toilet, chewing on the ends of her hair.

Mae shook her head. "He never remarried when Mom left." A nice way of saying that she'd faked her death, because once Mae started looking, it was as if clues intentionally popped up.

"Why would she do that?" Confusion wrinkled Lin's brow.

"I don't know." But Mae didn't appreciate it. A mother didn't have the right to keep a child, in this case *children*, away from their father. Plenty of parents divorced and shared custody. Not to mention, why lie? Their mother had had ten years to explain why their father still lived, and they couldn't see him. Ten years of silence.

Was it revenge? Mae wouldn't have called her mother petty, and yet, she'd read the stories. Knew how divorce made some people crazy. Mother had tried to avoid that by running away. It explained her paranoia.

But it didn't give her an excuse.

Mae wanted to meet her daddy. Which was why, in that bathroom, that same night, she'd sent him a message, an online search netting her a surprising email address.

She didn't expect a reply, and yet it came within the hour.

Dearest daughter, it fills me with immense joy to hear from you. Please, let us not waste any time and meet at once. Your choice of location and time. Bring your mother if you wish. Let us end this terrible separation. Your ever-loving father. Ronin.

It was a more perfect reply than she'd expected. Saying all the right things. Eloquent. Eager.

It filled Mae with hope. And fear. What if her father was disappointed when he met her? Then she felt guilt. Because she'd done something her mother wouldn't like.

How to tell her? Maybe she wouldn't tell her quite yet. She could communicate with her father, meet with him, take his measure, and ease the transition. Show her mother that she had nothing to fear.

Mae and Lin would never abandon her.

So, she felt quite confident in making arrangements to meet him in a public place. After all, there were people around. They could easily call for help.

Then again, why would she need aid? This was her father.

He'd been so happy that she wanted to meet. Claimed he was hopping on a plane at that very moment so he wouldn't be late to meet them.

A little too eager? Everything had moved faster than expected. Too fast. And now that Mae sat in a pizza shop, an old one in need of new paint, waiting for him to arrive, she couldn't help but eye the door and wonder if perhaps she'd made a mistake.

Then it was too late.

He came from behind, the murmur in the shop dying being her only warning. She noticed the four other people inside paying attention to a spot behind her.

As if in a dream, Mae pivoted on her stool and saw him.

Taller than expected. Handsome, even if the pictures didn't hint at the gray feathering his temples. His suit neat and unwrinkled. His expression smiling. "Hello. I am Ronin. You must be Mae and Lin. My daughters." He held open his arms.

Lin threw herself off the stool to hug him. Mae moved more slowly. She couldn't explain her trepidation. This was what she'd wanted.

She eyed the door. Then the still-silent restaurant.

Why did they all watch her father as if waiting for something?

"You don't greet your father?" The words sounded pleasant enough, and yet a glance at his face showed that his eyes were tight.

Angry? Or was that sorrow at her seeming rejection?

"Father." She sketched him a short bow before hugging him, Lin moving aside to make room for her twin.

There was none of the warm comfort she got from her mother or Aunt Joanna. Even Ted, for that matter.

Blame it on her nerves. She'd done it. Found her father. Good or bad, there was no turning back now.

Conversation in the pizza shop resumed as Father led them to a booth instead of the stools. It placed them in the window bordering the sidewalk, which made Mae fidget. What if her mother and Ted came strolling down this street and saw them?

Her father noticed. "What's wrong?"

"Nothing." Which was a lie. Hadn't her family had enough of those? "Mom doesn't know we came to see you."

"Probably for the best, given her decision to keep us separated." The words emerged tight and clipped.

"I'm sure she had a reason," Lin softly stated.

"There is no possible reason for a father to be kept from his children."

Mae almost objected. She could think of plenty of reasons, none of them very nice. Was their father that kind of man? The kind who hurt his family? She was beginning to wonder because, despite his apparent pleasant demeanor, she couldn't help but feel that he hid something.

He bought them each a Coke float, a glass of fizzing dark pop with a scoop of ice cream on top. He asked them a few mundane questions about their health and their upbringing. But it was when he asked about how they'd gotten to the island that Mae began to feel uncomfortable. Not so Lin.

"We're on a cruise."

"Really?" Ronin leaned forward. "And what's the name of your ship?"

"Princess something or other," Mae muttered, which described a good three or four vessels. But not theirs.

When Lin opened her mouth to correct Mae, she kicked her under the table, even as she smiled sweetly at their father. "We really should get back to the ship. We can't be late." Not for the departure, at least. Too late, she kind of wished she'd spent more time emailing her dad. He wasn't at all how she'd imagined. Not to mention, Mom would be so mad when she found out what Mae had done.

"You're not finishing the cruise," Ronin stated.

"Why not?" Lin asked, which was good because it saved Mae the trouble.

The smile on his lips held no warmth. "Because we're going home."

Lin still didn't understand. "Our house burned down."

"I know. I was the one who had the fire set." His grin widened. "Your home is now with me. Wherever I go. You go. *Daughters*."

The claim didn't inspire a warm and fuzzy feeling. "We live with Mom," Mae mumbled softly.

"Not anymore. I've missed out on ten years of your lives. That changes today."

"You can't just decide that. Custody agreements are made in courts, by a judge."

"Maybe in your country. But we're not in the United States. As your father, I am claiming you, as is my right."

Staring at him, Mae began to grasp her error in contacting him. *What have I done?*

Lin began to shake her head wildly. "I don't want to live with you. I want Mom."

"Then you'd better hope she chooses to return to me," Ronin said with a cruel twist of his lips.

Enough was enough. "I think this was a mistake." Grabbing Lin's hand, Mae hauled her sister as she dove out of the booth. They were young. Fast. If they could keep out of his reach, they'd make it to the ship where it was safe. Mom would protect them.

The plan might have succeeded, only the two people sitting by the table at the door stood and blocked her way. When Mae whirled, she noted that the other two customers were also on their feet, flanking their father.

A chiding click emerged from him as he approached. "How disappointing. And to think we were having such a pleasant reunion."

"You can't keep us."

"On the contrary. I can, and I will. And if I dangle you just right, I bet I'll snare your mother, too."

CHAPTER EIGHTEEN

THE TWINS WEREN'T in their room, and a quick check of the public areas didn't show them anywhere else either.

Macey was freaking, and Ted couldn't blame her. "He's taken them."

"You can't be sure."

"It's Ronin. I can feel it."

Looking around the tidy room, Ted didn't entirely agree. "How did he get past Joanna?"

"Drugged her, obviously."

"Why don't we wake her and find out?"

Macey had just the thing, a shot that, when injected, caused Joanna to open her eyes wide and gasp. "What the hell?"

"You tell me! Where are the girls?"

"What do you mean, they're right..." Joanna's voice trailed off as she took in the room and their faces. "Oh, shit. Those brats. They drugged me."

"Mae and Lin?" Macey scoffed. "They wouldn't."

"Don't be so sure. I knew something was up. Remember how I told you the girls weren't sick? I was right. The moment you were gone, they were pacing the room. Acting nervous and secretive. Lin especially. Lots of whispering going on."

"And you didn't think to ask them why?" Macey crossed her arms.

Joanna was having none of it. "Of course, I asked. They gave me some crap answer."

"This is my fault. I never should have left," Macey huffed.

"We can't automatically assume they're in trouble. They're curious young ladies, could be they wanted to go exploring without an adult."

"They wouldn't dare."

Joanna snorted. "Now, you're being naïve."

"What are you suggesting? That my girls drugged you so they could wander off on their own. That's ludicrous."

"Is it really?" Joanna pointed to a bottle of juice on the nightstand. "I assume that's how they drugged me. One minute, I was popping stomach pills and chugging the juice they gave me to wash it down. The next, you were waking me up."

"You don't know they drugged it. Could be someone else planted it."

Ted blinked at her. "You really don't want to believe it." He glanced at Joanna, who shrugged.

"She's blind where they're concerned."

"I know my girls," Macey snapped. "They wouldn't do something like this."

"Unless they had a good reason," Ted offered. "Let's pretend for a moment that they did put Joanna to sleep. Why? Where did they want to go that they figured we'd say no to?" he asked.

"I don't know. Ask her. She was the one with them before it happened." Macey glared.

"Don't look at me," Joanna stated. "I was outsmarted by a pair of ten-year-olds."

In Joanna's defense, they were pretty fucking smart.

"All this arguing isn't helping to find them. We need a plan."

Chances were they'd gone on an adventure, and they'd come back when they were good and done. However, they were attractive ten-year-olds. Too pretty. Without an adult to watch over them.

"They must have left a clue." Ted glanced at Joanna. "Were they on their tablets at all?"

"Yeah. Reading."

"I turned off their Wi-Fi," Macey remarked. "I wanted to make sure they didn't accidentally broadcast our location."

"Have you forgotten what you told me about Mae?"

It took a bit before Macey's expression changed as she had her lightbulb moment. "She won the junior female hacking tournament last year. But that was for kid stuff."

"And?"

Macey scrambled over the bed and snared the tablet from the nightstand. Locked. And after five wrong attempts, it flashed a permanent user locked out notification.

"Dammit." Macey flung it aside and eyed Lin's device.

"Before you start playing with it, maybe we should try something else."

"Like?" she snapped. She rubbed her worried brow. "Sorry. I know I'm being a bitch, but I can't help it. Something is wrong. I can feel it."

"Then let's slow down so we don't fuck this up. Because I assume you don't know Lin's password."

"No. It's not a word, though. It's a shape." She showed him the grid with the nine points.

"Can I have it for a second?" He held the tablet up and tilted it, trying to get a feel for the marks on the screen. While tapping left a distinct print, sliding a finger in a pattern often enough might just leave a mark. "I need a pen and paper."

In seconds, he had both and drew what he thought Lin might be using as a symbol. It looked like the letter G.

"I think this might be her symbol to get in."

"Try it." Macey hugged herself as he tried it, first drawing it from the top.

Failed. Then he did it in reverse from the bottom.

Failed.

"Let me try." Macey grabbed it and tried. Third fail. Two more, and they were done.

She glanced at the notebook on the nightstand, Lin's journal of thoughts. Written in big black letters was: *Do not open. Go away*. Macey redid the G but added a flourish at the end, just like the letter on the cover of the journal.

"I'm in!" she crowed. But her elation quickly faded as they began to read the conversation between the girls.

Ted kept reading when Macey turned away, stifling a sob with a fist in her mouth.

They painted a disturbing picture. The girls had learned about their father. Knew that Macey had lied, and Mae at least was pissed about it. An asshole would have said, "*told you so*." But he wasn't about to kick her when she was down. She knew she'd fucked up. Now, they had to fix things. I appeared as if the girls had made arrangements to meet their father. Problem was, their correspondence didn't say where. Just a time, already past.

Honk.

The boat gave a warning blare, the first one that said, "*get your ass moving!*" because the ship was about to leave port.

Macey's eyes widened. "We can't leave. What if they're on the island?"

"They could be on the ship, too," Joanna argued. "Doesn't say anything about their meeting place."

It didn't, but it would be harder for Ronin to sneak aboard. And if they were on shore, the danger was much greater. "Macey and I will stay on the island to look. Joanna, you search the ship, top to bottom."

There was no time to grab luggage. They sprinted back to the loading area, seeing people rushing up the gangplank harried along by cruise staff.

As they ran off the boat, sprinting down the gangplank, some of the crew tried to stop them. But Macey pushed past them. She'd gone into full-blown panic mode.

Had the girls truly gone to meet their father?

Please don't let the man kill them to make their mother pay for her alleged sins. Ted had seen that kind of thing too often. Sometimes by men he'd known in his military days. A few women succumbed, too. The mind liked to play tricks on those suffering from PTSD and mental stress.

Poor Macey's anxiety manifested especially hard when it came to her children. This had to be killing her.

Spilling onto the island, they raced away from the port. But, eventually, they had to slow since they didn't know where to go next.

Macey appeared to realize that as she wailed. "They could be anywhere."

Ding.

The chime on her phone took them both by surprise.

She held it out. "It's from Mae. She says to meet her and Lin at a pizza shop." There was an address attached. It also said to come alone.

As if Ted would allow that to happen. "Let's go."

He held her hand as the GPS map led them through the streets to one sitting on an incline. At the top of the hill, they could see the sign for the restaurant.

Ted yanked her in between two buildings.

"What are you doing?" She pulled free.

"We can't go rushing in."

"I need to find my girls."

"What if Ronin is in there?"

Her lips thinned, and she lifted the skirt of her dress

to show the harness on her thigh. "Then I guess I'll finally be a real widow."

"Are you really going to shoot Ronin in front of your daughters and witnesses? Because that's a surefire way of ensuring that you lose them permanently."

"Mother would spring me."

"If you're not killed first by the cops. We should split up. Ronin doesn't know me, so I could go through the front while you infiltrate the back."

"The message said to come alone."

"Because it's a trap."

"I know it is, but I can't take a chance. Not with my girls."

"What's your plan, then?"

Macey put a hand on his chest. "Stay here."

"No way. I'm coming with you."

She shook her head. "If Ronin even suspects that you and I are together, he'll kill you."

"Do you really think I'm going to just let you walk in there where that bastard can harm you?"

"Ronin might harm me, but he won't kill me. His pride will demand satisfaction."

He stared at her. "Do you seriously think I'm going to let anyone hurt you?"

"You have to let me go alone. I need to get to my girls."

"He might kill you."

"Possibly. But I doubt it." She glanced over her shoulder at the opening to the alley, and only yards away, the restaurant. "I always knew this day would come."

"You can't just give up."

"I'm not. But at the same time, there is no other choice. I need to be the one to go."

"Macey—"

She stepped close and cupped his cheeks. "You make me wish I'd said yes in high school when you asked me out."

"Why does it sound like you're saying goodbye?"

Her lips turned down. "Because even if I manage to escape with the girls, I'll never be free."

"I want to be with you."

"Me, too."

She kissed him. Her mouth tasted of strawberries, slick and sweet. It was a kiss of farewell.

He licked his lips, savoring her flavor. His tongue went numb, and his eyes blinked slowly as he watched her wiping her mouth with a rag and then reapplying some gloss. "Counter-agent," she whispered. "I'm sorry."

He wanted to speak, but everything was heavy. "What. You. Do?" he asked as he felt his knees buckling.

"I'm saving your life."

"No." A word whispered against the thick falling slumber. His eyes shut. When they opened again, it was night. He appeared to be in the same alley, now stripped naked. On the plus side, he still possessed all of his organs.

On the negative...

Macey was gone.

As were the girls.

Because he'd failed. Failed to protect.

The realization riled the demon that lived inside his head. The one that made him do bad things.

Bad. Bad. Things. For a moment, as he stumbled naked from the alley, his gaze slewed to a tavern, the noise of it spilling onto the street, promising alcohol to dull his senses. He could probably find some drugs too and make his misery vanish for a moment.

But where would that leave Macey and the twins?

At the mercy of a bastard. He needed to find them. Fast. But for that, he needed help. First, though...pants. A man with his dick and balls hanging out wasn't exactly inconspicuous.

This time of night, few clotheslines held any items. Still, he managed a sarong of sorts with a blanket left hanging over a rickety fence. Loins covered, he still lacked a weapon or a phone.

It was maybe a half-mile of aimless wandering from where he'd been dumped before he saw a guy wearing his shirt and shoes. Could it be that he had other items of Ted's, too?

He slipped into an alley and waited for the guy to pass before grabbing him, slamming him into a wall and growling, "I think you have some shit of mine."

The guy didn't have his phone, but he knew the fellow who did, and he took Ted to him once they'd chatted a while with fists.

Recovering his phone, shirt, and shoes, but still wearing a fucking blanket skirt, he placed his first call. "She left!" he barked the words into the phone as soon as Marie answered.

"What happened?"

He offered a quick explanation that left Marie cussing up a storm.

"That idiot!" Macey's handler huffed. "She should have waited for aid."

"Can you blame her? She panicked once she knew that her ex had the girls. What a clusterfuck." Ted raked a hand through his hair.

"He won't harm the girls." Marie sounded mostly certain. But there was a bit of hesitation.

He felt it himself. Along with a cold dread. "But he will hurt Macey."

"Most likely."

Anger boiled. "This could have been avoided if you'd just had him killed."

"We couldn't."

"What do you mean couldn't?" he snapped as he paced. "You're an agency of professional assassins."

"And we tried when we first extracted her. It resulted in two deaths and a third operative put in the hospital, who retired after. Each attempt resulted in abject failures. So, we stopped."

"Why didn't Macey engineer something? Isn't she supposed to be some kind of whiz? She could have concocted something to take him out without ever coming close if her reputation is true."

"Oh, it's true. But the thing is, love and hate are a complicated thing. Especially when children are involved."

"I don't understand."

"Let me put this more clearly for you. How do you kill someone's father? Could you kill let's say the twins' father?"

"Hell yeah," he quickly blurted. "The guy is scum."

"Let's say you did finish him. Would you tell Portia? The twins?"

He thought about looking them in the face and admitting what he had done. Would they thank him? He'd read the texts the girls had exchanged. Excited about meeting their dad. They'd gone in with high hopes. What if, for all his faults, the guy was a good father? What if the twins loved him?

Could he still kill the man?

"They'd be better off without him around."

"Yes, they would. Hence why we tried in the early years. However, as time passed, despite Portia's fear of Ronin, she could never bring herself to strike that final blow. Which meant, we couldn't act either."

"She should know better than to bring sentimentality into it."

"And yet isn't that what you're doing? You're determined to rush in and kill, kill, kill."

"He's a threat."

"Yes, but the true mission isn't his fate. It's that of Macey and the girls. We need to locate them and extract them in a way that harms no one."

"And how do you suggest we do that?"

"I don't know."

The three scariest words he'd ever heard.

CHAPTER NINETEEN

PORTIA REGRETTED DRUGGING TED, especially given the look of betrayal in his eyes. The good news was that it would last just long enough for her to get this meeting over with.

She didn't want to leave him helpless for long. Ted had left her no choice, though. She couldn't risk angering Ronin. Not with the girls possibly in his care.

She didn't believe for a moment that the message she'd received had come from Mae. Which meant that *he'd* sent it. If Ronin thought for one second that Ted was a threat...

Better that she did this alone. She'd survived Ronin's abuse once before when she was young and dumb and unable to defend herself. Stronger now, she knew he couldn't break her.

Brave words. Courageous thoughts. They lasted until Portia walked into the greasy restaurant and saw him again. She'd spent a decade picturing what she'd say if she ever came face to face with Ronin again. Most of her speeches were profane. Involved yelling. Tears, too.

Then she really looked at him. A man who hadn't aged much and stood as she entered. Even dared to smile.

A part of her wanted to scream. Shrink. Run away. It took effort to keep her shoulders straight as she scanned the restaurant for her daughters.

"Macey. You're looking beautiful, as always."

His voice should have repulsed. His face. Body. Everything should have been gross to her, but looking at him, he remained as handsome and smooth as ever. She dug her nails into her palms.

"Where are my girls? What have you done to my children?" The wrong thing to say.

His expression hardened. "*Our* daughters are currently indulging themselves in a villa I'm renting."

"You had no right to take them."

His brows lifted. "No right? On the contrary. Given your actions, I'm the only one with any rights. Faking your death, stealing my children, lying to them. To me. Once I'm done with you in court, you'll be lucky if you get to see pictures of them a few times a year."

She lunged for him. "How dare you?"

He caught her wrists and yanked her close. "I dare because they are my daughters, my blood. Just like you are my wife."

"No, I'm not."

"We're not divorced, my love. Nor am I widowed anymore. Instead, I have you back in my arms. Where you belong." The words had an ominous lilt.

"I'll kill you." She said it and meant it. She never should have hemmed and hawed over the years. Never should have wondered at the morality of killing the twins' father. A mistake, she realized now. An error she'd rectify.

Lucky for her, he'd not yet thought to have her searched. He didn't know about the gun strapped to the inside of her leg.

"You are welcome to try and kill me. Rumor has it you took out Chen."

"I've taken out more people than you can imagine."

"Have you really?" His smile stretched. "I look forward to hearing about your conquests."

"How about I show you?" She smiled sweetly.

"Or you could try being less tedious. Acting as if you are the aggrieved party. Given your subterfuge, my patience is stretched rather thin. It would be a shame if it snapped, and I took it out on someone."

"Go ahead and hit me." She lifted her chin, daring him. Maybe someone passing outside would see and call for help.

"Never said I wanted to strike you. We've just been reunited. Which is a cause for joy. As is becoming a new father. Although, I will admit, I'm already discovering that being a parent can be trying. Apparently, only one of us is a proponent of spare the rod, spoil the child, as you Americans would say."

The threat chilled her to the bone. "Don't you dare lay a hand on the girls."

"If you wish them to remain unharmed, then you will

behave. Be a proper wife and mother. Earn my forgiveness. Or they will suffer my wrath. Your choice."

It was the one threat she couldn't ignore. But she did have to wonder... "Why me? Why does it have to be me when you could have anyone?"

"It is exactly because I can have anyone that you must be the one to submit. Shaming me. Choosing to consort with another *man*." Ronin's lip curled. "The irony is, you can thank Grady for me finding out you're alive. He poked around somewhere he shouldn't have. Looking for someone who was supposed to be dead. But I'd always wondered. What if my wife hadn't perished in that crash? What if the ring found in the wreckage wasn't on her finger when it burned?"

"You suspected that I was alive?"

"More like hoped, my love." He said the term almost mockingly. "Which is why when it was brought to my attention that every single record of you had been removed, I created one subtle entry and had an electronic trace attached to it. Then, I waited."

The patience and thought behind it had her gaping. "You set a trap."

"More like cheese for a mouse. And someone took a nibble at it. I will admit, though, you did a most excellent job of concealing yourself. After ten years, I'd just about forgotten about the little trap I'd set. Funny how it takes only one thread to unravel everything."

"You could have just left us alone."

"Are you really going to blame me?" He pretended to be the injured party. "I will note that it was our daughters who reached out to me. Who asked to meet their father. Ironic that the very people you protected betrayed you."

Ronin still knew how to inflict the most pain with just a few words. It did hurt that the girls had gone behind her back and lied. But they'd only done it because she'd lied first.

"I want to see them."

"Say please."

She gritted her jaw. "Please."

"Not good enough." He pointed to the floor.

Her fists clenched. She knew what he wanted. For her to beg.

She wanted to tell him to fuck off.

She wanted to dive at his face and rip out his eyes.

She wanted her daughters most of all.

Her knees hit the hard concrete. She stared at his shoes rather than glare at his face as she said, "Please, Ronin. Let me see my girls."

"Only after you show me how much you've missed me."

He expected sex. How pathetic.

"Going to make me whore myself?"

He laughed. "You think highly of yourself. As I recall, your skills left much to be desired. No, my love, I won't need your tainted lips touching me. But you will show proper obeisance."

"I won't be your slave."

"Then I guess we're done." He walked past her, and she had no doubt that he'd leave and make sure she never saw her daughters again.

"Wait."

He paused.

She shuffled forward, her head bowed. "I'm sorry I left."

"Sorry...what?"

It soured in her mouth to say, "My love."

"Was that so hard?"

She couldn't help but glance at him, only to catch his triumphant smirk. He thought he'd won, and she'd wager that he believed her to still be the weak Macey of before. The woman who would bow at threats.

Let him think that.

Let him underestimate her.

She ducked her head again and bowed even lower, using the bend of her body to hide the movement of her hand as it slid under the skirt of her dress, reaching for the gun holstered to her thigh.

"I wouldn't try that if I were you," was his soft warning. "Shoot me, and one of the girls will die. I left orders with those guarding them. It's up to you. Is my death worth losing one of our children?"

"Bastard," she hissed.

"Hardly. But I am also not stupid like Chen. Attempt to harm me, and there will be repercussions. Now, if you're done testing me, shall we go? You might want to hurry to decide. I also left orders about the timeframe in which I expected to return. We're cutting it close."

She shot him an angry glare. "You'd truly kill your own daughters?"

"If one dies, I still have the other."

The coldness of the remark had her slumping. He'd won. She couldn't risk her daughters. "I'm coming." She rose to her feet. When he gestured for her to go ahead, she shuffled to the door and got into the car that pulled up outside.

Funny how in all her nightmares, not once did she ever walk to her doom of her own volition.

Reality proved most frightening of all.

20

THE TWINS

"RONIN IS NOT A NICE MAN," Lin declared less than twenty-four hours after they'd met him, and only after disabling the camera and microphone in their room. Who put listening and surveillance devices in a young girl's room? And recently, too. The plaster and concrete silt from their installation still dusted the dresser under it.

Despite Mae agreeing with her sister's assessment, she couldn't help but feel ornery about it. Because admitting that their father was a jerk, meant having to fess up that she'd been wrong. That perhaps Mother knew best. But she was still mad at her mom.

"He is exactly how a father should be. Well-dressed. Hard-working." Or so it seemed, given how he barked, and people listened. "He knows how to command." And possessed a stern mien, along with old-fashioned ideas like having the girls dress for dinner and waiting to be told to speak. Mae didn't have a hard time with that one as she went silent for most of the meal. However, Lin gushed about everything. It irritated

Father as they had sat at the formal dining table the night before. She could see it in the tic jumping by his eye.

Lin didn't get any of the subtle hints, but she did snap her mouth shut when Father finally barked, "Cease your useless prattling."

Mae's mouth opened. How dare he speak to her sister like that? How dare—?

He slewed a cold gaze in her direction, and Mae kept her lips sealed.

Even now, despite the camera being disabled—because Lin, being less than subtle, had actually removed it from the wall—she had to wonder if there was another watching. What if Father had more eyes and ears?

Lin either didn't think of it or didn't care. "You forgot to add that he's arrogant and just plain mean. Did you hear how he talks to the staff?" Trust Lin to be more worried about others than herself.

"He's an important man." Mae could think of a thousand excuses. Did any of them justify his behavior? Then again, perhaps it was because they didn't know each other. Strangers that had known each other less than a day. Perhaps over time, he'd soften?

"I don't like him. I want to go home." Lin's lower lip jutted.

"We don't have a home, remember? It burned down." Burned down on Ronin's orders. What kind of person did that?

The tears truly welled in her sister's eyes. "All our stuff is gone."

Mae had been doing her best to not think about that.

If she did, she might let out a never-ending scream. She had to remain strong, now more than ever. For her sister.

Because I screwed up.

"I want Mom." Lin's lips trembled.

"Me, too," Mae admitted. What had started out as an adventure had turned into a nightmare. "Let's find a way to call her."

"How? We left our tablets on the boat." With their handheld devices and some Wi-Fi, or a cell connection, they could have contacted her.

There didn't appear to be any phones lying around the villa. A lavish place of concrete walls layered over in many rooms with a textured plaster. The staff didn't say anything to the girls. Just brought them whatever they asked for. And chances were they reported to someone who would tell their father.

"We need to get our hands on something we can connect to the internet." If they asked for a device from the staff and claimed they needed it for entertainment, would they give the girls one? Maybe they should just try filching one. But that would require them running into someone carrying a phone.

"Come on," Mae said suddenly, rolling off Lin's bed. "Let's go outside for some air."

"I don't want to go outside," Lin pouted.

"Trust me. You want to go outside," Mae enunciated. Her sister was miserable, and Mae wasn't feeling too happy herself. Time to examine the problem and figure out a solution.

"You suck."

"I know." She dragged Lin down the long hall in the

wing with their adjoining bedrooms. The coral floors, preserved under a clear coat, let them walk barefoot without any jaggedness. At the end of the hall, patio doors led into a courtyard, walled all around, twenty paces by thirty paces. It provided a secure and beautiful garden surrounding a plunge pool, the greenery of the topiaries lush. A pair of lounge chairs flanked a short table. If they sat out here, someone would bring them a drink.

If they went for a swim, they'd find a towel for each of them folded by the edge. Someone was always watching. Despite their father's demeanor towards them, the girls received all kinds of pampering. Their treatment was luxurious, as were their rooms. A shared bathroom joined their bedrooms, both of them much bigger than the one they used to have.

There was a giant living room with a massive television. A dining room with way too many chairs. At various points throughout the house, armed men could be spotted in the halls, the windows not facing the courtyard electronically locked at all times. The girls had received a warning that they weren't to leave the house without permission.

A pretty prison.

As Lin flopped onto the seat, Mae glanced around, wondering where the camera was located. The climbing vines hid most of the cement-block wall to the second floor. A slight movement drew her attention to the man standing in shadows on the second-floor balcony. It ran around the entire space, and she'd wager there was a matching sniper concealed on the opposite side.

What kind of man required such intense security?

And the more disturbing thought, how would Mother manage to take them back? Because Mae had no doubt that Father had meant what he said. He was keeping his daughters. He had the power and wealth to do it.

Mae needed to get a message out.

She sat in the other chair and waited. Someone would arrive any second now with a drink. She could then ask for a tablet or phone to entertain herself. The worst that could happen was that they'd say no.

"I want to go outside. Somewhere other than this garden." Lin's petulance proved contagious.

Usually an epic sulker, Mae found herself in an odd position. "We could ask Father."

"Ask Father for what?" The sudden query had Lin squeaking as her father stepped out of the house, choosing a door that opened up behind them.

Mae craned and saw him approaching, alone. What ill luck. Or was it?

"I was just saying to Lin that we are getting behind on our schoolwork."

"Studies on vacation?" Father asked.

"Reading, mostly. We're trying to get through six classics each and do a comparison book report. Which I guess we won't finish since we don't have our tablets."

"Tablets are toys," Father scoffed.

"Mom didn't want us having laptops yet." A lie. They'd had some in their old house but had traveled only with their tablets.

"Your mother was obviously holding you back. A

child's education today must take into account the virtual aspect of it. Technology is the future."

"So, we can have a laptop?"

"You'll each get a pair, but I expect to see results. You will present the book report when completed. In a timely manner."

"Yes, Father." Mae ducked her head and hid a smile. That had been much easier than expected.

"With that done..." Father tucked his hands behind his back and switched to a Chinese dialect. "How fare my daughters today?"

She replied. "We are well, thank you. And yourself?"

"Busy. I've been preoccupied with a special project that I believe is about to come to fruition."

"I am pleased by your success," Mae said, knowing how to handle their father. But Lin wasn't in the mood to stroke his ego.

"I want to talk to Mom," Lin exclaimed in English.

Rather than say no, their father smiled. "You'll speak to her once she and I come to an understanding. Which I believe is very close."

"You've talked to her?" Mae exclaimed. What she didn't ask was if their mom was mad.

"I've been speaking with her at length. As a matter of fact, she's in this house." He casually relayed that bombshell.

Forget acting. Mae blurted, "Where?"

"Not a place you're allowed to visit yet. Right now, she's rethinking her choices."

A crease of worry marred Lin's brow. "You're not going to hurt Mom, are you?"

Hurt? Mae's eyes widened. Surely, he wouldn't. Then again, look at his actions thus far.

He managed to appear offended. "Do you question my honor?"

"No." Lin worried her lower lip.

"When you address me, it is to be as Father or sir. We are not peasants."

"Yes, Father. Sir. Sorry."

"Stand up when you apologize. Really, how many times must you be told?"

Mae rose along with her sister. It had never occurred to her that he'd require them to stand when he entered a room. Just how crazy was he? The difference between him and Ted proved astonishing. Ted never played these kinds of mean games with them.

Lin's head ducked, and Mae might have thought her cowed if she'd not seen her clenched fists. "My apologies, *sir*." The inflection completely ruined it, but Father accepted it.

"Perhaps you require some quiet and alone time like your mother. To reflect."

Wait, was he talking about separating them? Mae had to nip that idea in the bud. How? "I'm sure you and Mom have lots to talk about. We just miss her. A lot. But we know you have our best interests at heart. Father." She remembered to add that at the end.

He appeared somewhat mollified. His frown eased, and yet she shivered at the look in her father's eyes. "Perhaps it is time to reunite you. To show her what her actions cost."

"I'm sure she's very sorry about what she did."

"She will be."

"Don't you dare hurt her," Lin exploded, and before Mae could stop her, her sister had thrown herself at their father, pummeling him with little fists.

He glanced down and then shoved her, sent Lin flying, hard enough that she tripped over the edge of the pool and fell in.

"Lin!" Mae shrieked.

Her sister swam to the surface, wide-eyed and clearly scared. But it was the terror when two of the armed guards came outside and told Lin to go with them that was the worst.

Father's orders. Lin needed to be punished. Which, apparently, consisted of placing her in solitary. Just like their mother. Mae would have joined them if she'd not held her tongue. She didn't act. Didn't speak. Hoped Lin would understand that she had to remain free so she could act. Because only she could rectify this.

It was a full four hours before she got to see Lin. Two more after that before they saw their mother.

The last thirty-some hours hadn't been very kind.

Ronin sent a minion to fetch Mae and Lin. Which meant a quick brushing of their hair and straightening of their clothes. He didn't tolerate untidiness. Mae closed the lid on the laptop. Father had come through with excellent quality machines, ones that she'd been putting to good use.

They entered the parlor, a place of white wicker furniture and a peaked ceiling made of polished wooden planks. A nice room, but the best thing in it was sitting in a chair.

Mom's face brightened at the sight of them.

"Girls, are you okay?"

"Mommy," Lin exclaimed, running for her. Mae held back. Suddenly ashamed of her actions, especially when she saw the sunken hollows below her mother's eyes and the red mark on her cheek.

What happened? Had Father hit her? He'd not struck Mae or Lin. He knew better punishments.

"As you can see, my love, *my* daughters are fine, and this despite your attempts to keep us apart. A heinous crime, wouldn't you say?"

"My fault, not theirs. Don't hurt them."

"Or what?" Father taunted. "I will remind you that you aren't in a position to demand anything. Or has your time in solitary not been enough to remind you of your rightful spot? Perhaps you need more time alone to reflect."

"No," Lin squeaked. She still held onto their mom and sniffled. "I wanna go home."

"Your home is with me." Flatly said by Ronin. "Tell them, my love."

Mae prepared to hear her mother deny it. After all, she'd never cowered before anyone. Even Ted knew better than to make her mad.

Mother's head ducked, her gaze not meeting theirs. "You're staying with your father."

"No." Lin backed away from their mother, her lips trembling and eyes brimming with betrayal.

"I'm sorry, but we have to do as he says."

There was something terrifying about seeing her

mom conceding a fight. Mom always told them to never stop trying. Yet she appeared to have given up.

Or she was scared.

Mae glanced at Father, who'd reached out and grabbed Lin. Tight. Hard enough that her sister grimaced.

He's hurting her. Mae bristled.

This was all her fault.

She had to fix it.

Sometimes, it was good that adults underestimated them.

But right about now, Mae needed a grown-up to save them. And she could think of only one person she trusted.

CHAPTER TWENTY-ONE

IT HAD BEEN ALMOST two days since Macey and the girls had disappeared. Marie believed that they remained in the islands. She just couldn't be sure which one. Ronin's private jet remained in China, the decoy sitting, still meaning they could be anywhere.

Macey might be dead.

Which might be why Ted was a tad too eager when his phone rang, the number unknown. Answering it beat staring at the mini bottle of booze sitting on his little fridge.

He'd not cracked the seal on it. Not yet. But if he didn't find Macey and the girls soon...

"Are you ready to move out?" Marie's voice said without any preamble.

He almost fell off the bed in the motel room he'd rented, the floral pattern of the comforter hideous enough to hide any stain. "You've got a location."

"I do. It would seem the twins are a tad disillusioned with their father and contacted me. They've provided coordinates. He's actually not very far. Holed up in a villa on a nearby mountain."

"Is Macey okay?"

"She's alive." Hesitantly spoken.

"He's hurt her." He growled the statement, and the hand holding the phone almost crushed the casing.

"The important thing is, she's alive," Marie repeated more softly.

"What of the girls?"

"They are fine, physically. Lin received solitary as some punishment, but he hasn't laid a hand on them."

"Thank fuck." Ted closed his eyes. "Soon, they won't have to worry about him. Once he's dead—"

"You're planning to kill him?" Marie interjected.

"If the opportunity presents itself, yes." It seemed rather obvious to him.

"You do understand that doing so might mean you won't be allowed in Portia's life afterwards."

He didn't question how the woman knew that they were involved. "I'll be doing them a favor."

"You'll be killing the twins' father."

"He's scum."

"He's still their father. And by killing him, you might make him a martyr for those girls."

Ted could see where that might lead Marie to believe that Portia might not want him in her life. Still... "I'll take that chance." Because by killing Ronin, he'd be doing the world a favor, and keeping the people he cared about safe.

It might cost him his only chance at happiness, but he'd pay the price. He understood how Macey felt when

221

she said that her life couldn't compare to her daughter's. In his case, his happiness seemed a paltry thing in comparison to theirs.

"You can't go in guns blazing. We don't want to accidentally shoot those we're trying to save," Marie warned.

"If you're worried about friendly fire injuries, don't. I never miss."

"If you're going to go off mission, then let me know now because my primary objective is getting Portia and the girls out safely."

"Mine, too. Don't worry." Left unsaid was that once they were out of the line of fire, Ted was handling the Ronin situation, once and for all.

CHAPTER TWENTY-TWO

PORTIA HAD BEEN RELEASED, but only because Ronin trusted that his threats would keep her in line. He was correct. She wouldn't act unless she knew the girls would remain safe.

But it wasn't easy biting her tongue. Especially when she saw the disappointment in Mae's face. Then the guilt. Which wasn't as bad as the sly expression. She knew that look, the one that said her kid was plotting. And that brain...who knew what Mae would think up.

However, she was only a child. She didn't understand just how vile Ronin could be. He was a master manipulator. He knew how to hurt her. Putting her alone in a room with the hurricane shutters blocking the window. Clocks removed. No sound. No people. Nothing but herself and her thoughts.

But she'd endured it. She wouldn't crack, wouldn't give in to his mind games. She'd outplay him instead.

However, she'd almost lost it when she saw her girls. Poor Lin, trembling and afraid. Mae...what did she plot?

Portia had to stop her before she did something that drew her father's wrath, which meant obeying him when he said to dress nicely for dinner.

Opening the closet, she noticed that it now held clothes rather than empty shelves. She chose a demure black dress, the kind that went over her knee with long sleeves and a square neckline, no cleavage. Some men might like curve-hugging and low-cut. Not Ronin.

Fully dressed, she rapped on the door. It opened, and a man stuck his face inside. "Ready?"

She nodded, not trusting herself to reply.

As she was herded down the hall, she caught movement and turned to see Lin, watching silently from behind a pillar that rose to the high, arched ceiling in the great room. She offered an exaggerated wink.

Why was her child winking?

Portia might have stopped to ask, yet her escort kept moving her along. Past the vast open space and through the formal dining space into a more private dining area. More of a lounge, with a table set for two, and a divan by a not-often-needed fireplace.

Ronin stood as she entered, always a perfect gentleman, all the better to hide the monster inside.

"My love, you are ravishing." He approached and grabbed her hand, drawing her to the table and helping her take her seat.

She tucked her hands into her lap lest she grab a knife and stab him. Her girls. She had to think of them. Get them to safety first, then she'd handle Ronin.

"Husband." She smiled sweetly. Pity her sleeping

gloss had been lost with her purse of toys. But a household such as this one would be well stocked with things she could use.

"It is good you've come to your senses."

"As if you gave me any choice." She spread a napkin on her lap. Took note that there were no guards stationed inside the room, or outside on the balcony, at least that she could see. Thick curtains framed the doors, and they shifted slightly in a slight breeze.

"From here on out, your choices are simple. Obey me, and your life can be luxurious."

"And if I don't, you'll hurt me or the girls."

"Probably the dumber one. Until you've given me another heir, a male this time, the obedient one will serve."

"Leave them alone." She couldn't listen to the threat and not speak.

"Testing my patience already, my love?" He arched a brow.

"More like wishing I'd had the courage to kill you ten years ago."

"As if you could murder me now," he sneered. "Go ahead and try. Do it." He pointed to the knife in front of her. "Take it and stab me, slice me. After all, it's not as if you haven't already hurt me enough."

She kept her hands tucked. "Don't you dare play the victim."

"I have every right. You left. You stole my children."

"You're a control freak."

"I was your husband."

"That didn't give you the right to hurt me." Even worse than the bruises of the flesh, the hematomas of the mind lingered the longest.

"You should have asked for a divorce."

"You would have said no," Portia blurted.

"You're right, I would have refused, and after the children were born, I'd probably have had you entered into a program to deal with your obviously hormonal mental lapse."

She pressed her lips together. "I don't want to be your wife."

"You don't get a choice."

"Yes, she does. And so do we." Mae stepped out from behind the drapes and eyed her father. "You're not a very nice person."

"I don't need to be nice. But I will be obeyed. Return to your room. At once. It would seem you require the same lesson as your sister when it comes to obedience."

But rather than listen, Mae moved closer. "You know, for a long time, I suffered under the misconception that I required a father. I wanted one so badly, and when I found out you were alive, I couldn't wait to meet you. In my mind, I'd built you into something grand. But it turns out you're"—she eyed him in a way that showed he left her unimpressed—"disappointing at best."

His face twisted. "You dare insult me?"

"Mom says I should always tell the truth, which is hypocritical coming from her." Mae rolled her eyes. "But, sometimes, she is right. You're not a very good person, but I am. Which is why you get a second chance."

Portia blinked as her daughter took on a maturity that had taken her much longer to find.

"What are you babbling about?"

"You've been a very bad man, Father." Mae shook her head. "Which is why you're being arrested."

"By whom?" he sneered. "Not that it matters. Any charges levied against me will get tossed by my lawyers." Ronin was so blasé about it as he stated what he believed was the simple truth and took a sip of his wine.

"Might be kind of hard to have the case dismissed with the evidence I provided," Mae declared, leading Portia to seesaw between pride and terror. Oh no, she hadn't.

She had.

"I've emailed a few international organizations with details of your crimes. Money laundering. Drugs." She shook her head. "You made it so easy for me to find."

It astonished Portia just how much she'd underestimated her child.

"You lie."

"Do I? How about you ask them." Mae eyed the ceiling, and it was then that Portia heard it, the whup-whup of helicopter blades. More than one. A flash of movement outside, and Mae's expression turned smug.

It dawned on Portia what Mae had done. "You called a SWAT team? Are you insane?" Portia might have yelled it, whereas Ronin spat, "You little bitch!"

Mae appeared to have factored many things into her plan. How to take her father by surprise, how to ensure that the case was airtight, but she'd never planned for the one thing that happened.

Ronin attacked Mae. He threw himself at her, hands outstretched, and Portia could only scream because she couldn't move fast enough to intervene. Ronin hit her daughter and slammed her into the floor.

Mae didn't get back up.

CHAPTER TWENTY-THREE

TED ROARED, a primal sound as he saw Mae go down. He'd just rappelled out of a helicopter—which was a blast from the past—and hit the ground running. He aimed for the patio doors, where he could see his target. Saw the fucker hitting a child.

Marie's warning to go slow went right out of his head. Danger. Danger. Instinct took over, and he yelled, "Hey, you ugly coward. Why not pick on someone your own goddamned size?"

Hearing Ted, Ronin rolled from Mae and stood, bouncing on the balls of his feet, fingers beckoning. "You want to fight, then let us fight."

The guy wanted to do a hand to hand competition? The butt of the gun by his side was already gripped in Ted's hand. It would be so easy to draw it and shoot.

Kill Ronin, a man he probably wouldn't have many nightmares about. It would solve so many problems. But then he looked at Mae. Tucked against Macey, her eyes wide with fear.

"Don't kill him. We have to find Lin first."

"Where is she?"

Ronin smiled. "Probably dead by now. My staff is very good at following orders."

"I'm not dead." Lin stepped out from behind the other drape and ran to her mother.

Anger twisted Ronin's face. "I'll deal with you in a moment. First, to teach this one a lesson."

Ronin dove at him, hands slashing, feet moving, making Ted realize that he wasn't the only one who'd trained in the arts.

He ducked and weaved, spending most of his time defending rather than attacking. Outside, they could hear the crack of gunfire. A scream as a stray shot entered the room and shattered a glass on the table distracted enough that Ronin landed a blow to Ted's jaw.

Ted reeled. The other man took advantage, taking his moment of inattention to pound him, over and over, to the point where he could only put his arms in front of his face to block and defend.

"Leave him alone."

Macey was the one to rescue him, the chair she swung knocking Ronin aside. The man rose, seething, bleeding from his temple, and somehow holding Ted's gun.

Fuck.

Her eyes widened.

The girls screamed.

Ted scissor-kicked and caught Ronin as he fired, jerking him. The gun cracked a moment before Ronin hit the floor, hard enough that his head bounced.

In a flash, Ted straddled him and had the gun in hand. It would be so easy now to end it.

He sensed more than saw the gazes focused on him. Remembered what Marie had said.

Can I really shoot their father in front of them?

Glancing at their wide eyes, the answer almost hurt.

Ted sighed. "I need some cuffs." He made do with the tassels Macey ripped from the cushions on the couch. He trussed Ronin up like a hog for the spit, and then leaned back on his heels.

A moment later, his choice was rewarded as two small bodies hurtled at him for a hug, then a third joined, her arms stretching wide.

Later, he might regret not killing Ronin. But right now, with Macey in his arms, and the girls tucked on either side, he felt pretty damned good about it.

CHAPTER TWENTY-FOUR

THE DAY ENDED BETTER than it had started.

Much better. For one, she was reunited with her girls.

Poor Mae, though, she sported bruises on her throat, and sounded quite hoarse when she spoke. She claimed that she was fine. But Portia had to wonder. Ronin had attacked Mae. His own daughter.

A natural reaction would be to get scared and be freaked out. Instead, Mae observed the people moving around the villa. Some of them she knew, like Meredith, and Carla—who'd had the baby and taken a year off, but came on the mission when she heard that Portia was in trouble.

There were some men roaming around, too, Bad Boy agents who'd coordinated with KM to send in a rescue force. Because Mae had known exactly who to call the moment she'd cracked the laptop's firewall.

She'd called her grandma.

Smart girl. Of course, Mae didn't know yet that the agents roaming the villa cleaning up the mess weren't an actual police force. Nor did she realize that her mother was anything more than what she appeared.

They did, however, believe that Ted was a super-spy agent, and were more enamored of him than ever.

"Are we going to finish our cruise?" a raspy Mae asked as they got into the van that would drive them to a resort.

She appeared fine. Too fine. Meaning she probably hid her true feelings.

Portia certainly did. Inside, she was a tumultuous mess. Coming face to face with Ronin, she'd not known how she would feel. Angry, yes. Murderous, too. But she'd not expected the sadness.

If only Ronin could have been a better man. Someone with some scruples and respect for friends, family, a spouse.

But he chose to be an asshole, never realizing that he caused his own misery. Had he been nicer to his daughters, they probably wouldn't have conspired to have him arrested.

Ronin was going to jail.

After a lengthy trial, that was. BBI and KM were, at this very moment, delivering him to the American authorities. Once they had Ronin in custody, they'd place him in the tightest security prison they had.

It wasn't how she'd pictured this ending, and yet, it worked. The girls wouldn't have to live with the guilt of his death. And as time passed, they'd move past what had happened.

"Mom?" Mae queried.

"What?" She blinked, completely lost.

"You didn't answer. Are we finishing our vacation?"

Portia shook her head. She couldn't handle the stress of more relaxation time. "No more cruising. Tomorrow, we'll be getting on a flight headed for home."

"What home? We have nothing." The reminder had Portia digging the heels of her hands into the sockets of her eyes. Pressing.

An arm went around her. "You have each other. Me, too, if you want me."

The words had her eyeing Ted. "Why would you want to stay?"

"Because you're still the same awesome girl I used to crush on in high school."

"I'm technically a married woman."

"Easy enough to hire a lawyer and fix that."

"With Ronin alive, the threat remains."

The girls sat in the rear seat, meaning that Ted, beside her in the middle row, could lean close and whisper, "Now that he's in jail..." He didn't have to finish that sentence.

She could technically finish things anytime now. She glanced over her shoulder at the girls, heads together, a laptop shared between them. She wouldn't kill him quite yet. They'd had enough shocks lately.

The resort didn't act surprised at all to see a family arriving late in the evening. Soon, they were ushered to a family suite, and no one argued as the girls went into the smaller bedroom with the twin beds. It only had one door and a window with no entry from the outside. Portia had checked.

She held each of her girls tightly and kissed them. "I love you."

"Love you, too, Mommy," Lin replied.

Whereas Mae sobbed. "I'm so sorry."

Portia hugged her daughter tighter. "No. Don't you dare apologize. I should have told you. Should have handled things better than I did."

"Is Father going to die in jail?"

The query froze Portia, especially because she'd already entertained thoughts about how it could happen. Food was taking a chance someone else would eat it. Undetectable poison on the toothbrush was a surer way.

"Of course, he won't die in jail. Why would you even ask?"

Mae lifted her head and said quite solemnly, "Epstein didn't kill himself."

Portia gaped. "What?"

The expression on her face was utter innocence. I said I know Daddy is a bad man, but I don't want him dead. Be sure you tell Grandma to not kill him. And Aunt Carla."

"I—um—"

It was Lin who confirmed what Portia feared. "When I grow up, I'm going to be a KM agent, too."

Mae snorted. "You can't join unless you're having a baby. I'm never having kids. I'm going to join Bad Boy instead."

"That's for boys only," Lin sassed with a roll of her eyes.

"Then I'll get them to start a girl agency."

The twins continued bickering as Portia closed the

door between the rooms, but she smiled. Despite everything that had happened, they were already adapting.

She heard a snicker and turned to see Ted lounging on the bed. "When do we their special agent training?"

"This isn't funny," she whispered. "I never wanted them to know what I did."

"Why not? You just became the coolest mom ever. You're not only a scientist, you're also a secret agent. Is it any wonder they want to grow up to be just like you?"

"I'm not that great."

"You seem perfect to me. Which is why I probably ain't got the right to ask, but I'm not a coward, so I am anyhow. Macey, Portia, or whatever name you choose next, I know things are a little crazy right now. And scary, too. But I'm really hoping you'll let me give you a hand with whatever comes next."

"I don't know if I'm ready to get married."

"Whoa, honey." He held up his hands. "Me either. I was talking more along the lines of getting to know each other. Giving you a hand moving into a new place."

"Moving furniture and putting up art with the occasional sleepover."

"Maybe more than occasional?" Queried with a boyish grin. "In other words, will you be my girlfriend?"

"Seriously?" she asked, arching a brow.

"Never more."

She eyed Ted, a guy who'd freely admitted that he used to be an asshole. Maybe not mobster level, but according to him, he'd done some bad shit. However, he'd chosen to turn his life around. To become a better person.

A man she felt like she could count on. Who respected her and her girls.

The kind of man she wouldn't mind having by her side.

She began to strip, and his expression turned heavy-lidded and smoldering.

"We have to be quiet," she whispered. They didn't have the hum of the ship's engines to hide some of the noise.

"Try not to scream," he declared with a naughty wink.

"Maybe I should sleep somewhere else, then," she teased.

"Like hell." He bounded off the bed and stalked toward her, already shirtless, his pants hanging low on his hips.

Oh, hell yes. She couldn't help but clench as lust filled her. As he stalked closer, she took tiny steps back until her butt hit the wall. Standing still, her body turned taut with anticipation.

He stopped not even an inch from her. He reached out to cup her jaw. "You're sleeping with me."

"Doesn't sound like you're asking."

"Are you going to tell me to leave?"

"No." She nuzzled her cheek into his hand. "But what you're asking... What if it doesn't work?"

"You mean what if I'm like Ronin and won't let you go?" His thumb stroked over her bottom lip. "Loving you means never doing anything that would cause you distress. My feelings don't matter."

"They do." She rocked forward against him. Cupped

his whole face with her hands. "You make me feel things. And it scares me."

"It scares me, too. But maybe together, we can conquer that fear."

Maybe they could.

There was no denying that she wanted him. Wanted this man who made her feel every inch a woman. She leaned up and kissed him. A light embrace that quickly turned carnal as his arms came around her. He drew her up on tiptoe so that he might properly plunder her mouth. Given that he held her up, she let her hands roam the bare skin of his upper body, stroking the velvety flesh over hard muscle, tenderly rubbing the scars.

She had been telling the truth when she said that he scared her. Because she felt things so strongly with him. Wanted so much.

It made her frantic. She pulled away from him and removed the damned dress she still wore. Underneath, matching black lace bra and panties. She would have removed them, too, but he growled, "No, keep them on."

She expected him to return her to his embrace. Instead, he whirled her around and pressed her cheek against the wall. His thick body pressed in from behind. He ground himself against her, and even with his pants buttoned, she felt the hard length of him.

She wiggled, and he grunted. Grasping her hands, he drew them above her head and growled, "Hold onto the wall."

The order only served to heighten her excitement. She obeyed, keeping her palms flat against the concrete.

A hand curved around her waist and drew her pelvis away from the wall. On instinct, she tilted her buttocks.

"Mmm." He hummed as his hand slid from her waist to snare the band of her underpants. He dragged them over her cheeks and kept tugging until they fell down her legs to pool at her ankles. It was simple enough to lift a foot and step out of them.

Only then did he nudge her legs apart. For a moment, he loomed against her, his body hot and hard at her back, his hand returning to cup her from the front, palming her mound and making her shiver.

His lips managed to part her hair to find the lobe of her ear as he traced her damp slit with his finger.

"Oh."

His touch proved light yet she quivered. She could feel the heat and moisture pooling between her legs. One stroking finger became two, the digits parting her nether lips and dipping into her sex. Penetrating her. Pumping, in and out.

Cheek pressed against the concrete, Portia did her best to hold in her moan. She couldn't make noise.

But it felt so good.

She squirmed, her breathing hitched as he pumped her with his fingers. Her hips rocked as he thrust, stroking her over and over in a rhythm that built into pleasure.

He suddenly dropped to his knees behind her, his hands gripping her cheeks to spread her so that he might replace fingers with tongue.

A strangled moan escaped her. This was torture. With a deft tongue, he traced her sex, slipping between her lips, flicking against her clit and then sucking it, pinching it with his lips until she clawed at the wall and practically sobbed.

He teased her, pleased her, brought her to the edge, and then stopped. He got her to the point where she was a quivering mess.

She finally sobbed, "I can't take anymore."

His words rumbled against her sex. "Then come."

"I want you inside me."

A shudder rocked his frame. "I won't make it inside you if you keep talking dirty like that."

He stood, and she heard the rustle of fabric as he removed his pants. She wiggled her hips impatiently.

"Gonna kill me," he grumbled, but softly. His hand once more curved around her waist, and her ass arched towards him. She parted her legs enough that he could probe her with the tip of his cock. He teased her.

But she didn't want to be teased anymore. Suddenly ducking and whirling, she faced him, grabbing his surprised face to plant a kiss. Her leg lifted and wrapped around his hip. It took a bit of wiggling from them both to get him in the right spot, and still, the angle wasn't quite right. She was too short.

"Lift me," she demanded.

A hand on each cheek, he complied. Finally, he fully sheathed himself. She sighed in pleasure as she felt every delicious inch of him. He stretched her, and she squeezed him. Slowly at first, he began to move, his hips making a thrusting motion. But gravity had her firmly planted on his dick, so all he did was grind deeper.

So deep, he hit a sweet spot. She clenched even

tighter. And tighter. She rocked, bounced, moved against him, wanting more of that friction. More of that...

"Oh—" The scream started to erupt, and he caught it with his mouth. Startled her into panting silence as her orgasm rippled. Shook her. Wrung her with intensity that left her limp.

He panted just as heavily but didn't drop her, although he moved quickly to the bed and collapsed on it, with her on top.

"I think I might love you," she whispered, her cheek on his chest, listening to the steady thump of his heart.

"I've always loved you," was his soft reply.

Exhaustion and satiation pulled them into sleep, a slumber without nightmares or sweats. It ended too early as they woke to the twins arguing at the foot of the bed.

"If it weren't for me, we'd still be stuck."

"If it weren't for you, Father would have never kidnapped us," Lin mocked.

"I fixed it."

"You sent out a coded message to Grandma. Wooo. Hoo." Lin waggled her head and sassed with her hands on her hips.

"I also found the evidence to have him arrested where he could get the help he needs," huffed Mae.

"Help? What help?" Ted asked.

Mae turned, matter-of-fact as she said, "Father obviously suffers mentally, has a certain Napolean syndrome. With proper guidance, he should learn to control his impulses and not want to rule the world."

Portia didn't feel the need to point out that no amount of therapy would help Ronin.

"And just in case he doesn't, I got his will changed to make us his heirs," Lin boasted, the mic drop moment of the whole conversation that had them gaping.

"You did what?" Ted exclaimed.

"What's the use in being his heirs if he's alive?" Mae scoffed, only to narrow her gaze. "You better not be thinking of killing Father just because you like Ted more."

"Of course, not," Lin exclaimed. "But given he's incarcerated and mentally incapacitated at the moment, an executor for his estate will be appointed. We'll have some say in that."

"With the right person, we could turn Father's empire around into one for good," Mae mused aloud. Portia wanted to groan.

Ted simply stretched, and the girls stopped arguing. But rather than eye his bare chest with interest like Portia did, in tandem, they said, "Hey, Ted, wanna play Mario Kart with us?"

It turned out he did.

And when the three of them had a burping contest later on, Portia had a cry in the bedroom. Happy tears.

Maybe it was time for her happily ever after.

EPILOGUE

SQUEALS of laughter drew her to the yard. A big one with trees and a swing set. Ted had insisted that they needed one, and a tree fort. The lumber for that had been delivered only the day before. Their dining room table even housed plans to put in a pool.

A few months ago, she would have laughed and said, *"Why, who will use it?"*

But that was before her girls remembered that they were still children.

Apparently, it took a grown man who'd never stopped being young to remind them. Portia leaned against the doorframe and watched her husband racing around the yard. They'd married in a very small ceremony where Marie was her matron of honor, and her sisters the brides-maids, with her girls as flower and ring girl.

Given that they'd relocated to Texas, Ted wore only swim shorts now, his chest bare, his scars still vivid slashes on his skin—a reminder of his past. Like her mental wounds, they would fade over time. Already, she stressed less. She'd even relaxed enough the other day to have a nap in the afternoon rather than work.

She. Napped.

Ted could be directly blamed for her new attitude and ease with life. The man balanced her crazy.

And then there was the thing driving her crazy in a good way. Her girls, currently in one-piece swimsuits as they chased Ted with water guns, spraying him, Ted protesting and laughing that they were ganging up on him.

When he dove for the hose, the girls shrieked and ran away. He uttered a fake evil laugh and chased after.

It brought a smile to her lips. Such a good man.

My man.

Her hand dropped to her tummy, just as he turned to look at her. His gaze dropped. Then rose.

He stumbled to a standstill and mouthed, "Are you?"

She nodded.

While he was distracted, Mae snuck up and yanked the hose out of his hand, turning it on him.

But he didn't care. He strode through that cold stream, smiling from ear to ear. He swung her into his arms, then around and around until she gasped, "I am going to puke on you."

Setting her down on her feet, he eyed the girls and said, "You're going to be—"

"Big sisters. We know." Mae rolled her eyes. "Took you long enough to figure it out."

"When can we tell him it's twins?" Lin asked, eyeing Portia.

"Two babies." He swayed on his feet.

The girls dropped their weapons and supported him, one on each side as they said in tandem, "Don't worry, Daddy. We'll help."

His gaze misted as he said, "My girls."

Portia's was even damper as she murmured, "My life."

The End

For the moment, that's it for the Killer Moms, but you never know... I might just be tempted to see how deadly a Dance Mom or a Unicorn Mom can be.

Looking for more Eve Langlais romantic suspense?

Check out Bad Boy Inc.